"Heading south through Keston o[n the] Westerham road, John Fowler swi[tched] on his radio for the news bulletin. Cassius Clay, he learned, was having hysterics on the eve of his fight with Liston. (Who wouldn't?) The Foreign Secretary had suggested at Geneva that everyone should burn certain weapons and put observers in each other's countries. (The weapons were obsolete; observers were already there, classified as diplomats or spies.) A circus, moving out of its winter quarters to some place near the coast and passing through Southborough in Kent *(South-borough?)* had mislaid a lion; local residents were warned to keep children and pets indoors until someone shot it.

"*Southborough.* That was just north of Tunbridge Wells, a stone's throw east of Speldhurst. . . ."

This is a novel about John Fowler, his eight-year-old son Andrew, an escaped lion, and a thoroughly delightful cast of characters, young and old, including Andrew's dearly loved and recently deceased grandfather.

Lionheart is rich in the qualities that make certain works of fiction stand head and shoulders above the rest. It is a short book but a book to cherish — witty, literate, suspenseful, and altogether credible.

1942 and later served in them in the North Sea and Far East.

After the war he learned Russian and served in Germany as naval liaison officer with Red Army units. In 1949 he resigned his commission and emigrated to South Africa, where six years later he started working for a group of London publishers. He returned in 1959 to live in England. Mr. Fullerton is married and has three sons.

LIONHEART

By the same author:

THE WAITING GAME

LIONHEART

by
ALEXANDER FULLERTON

W · W · NORTON & COMPANY · INC ·
New York

Library of Congress Catalog Card No. 65-25934

PRINTED IN THE UNITED STATES OF AMERICA

3 4 5 6 7 8 9 0

LIONHEART

I

WHEN HE WOKE, Andrew Fowler was truly awake at once and aware of the light behind the curtains which moved very gently in the early morning breeze; light filtered by the curtains streaked and patterned the low, creased ceiling, spread and shifted and accentuated the uneven plaster surface. The house was four hundred years old and there was hardly an even surface or a straight edge in it; the bed the boy lay in now—staring up at the light patterns on the ceiling and blinking as the curtains swayed—was propped up, on the side away from the wall, with wooden blocks under its legs.

Andrew had helped his father make the blocks, tightening the vice for him when he wanted it tightened, handing him the tools, even doing some of the sandpapering himself. There'd been a lot of small jobs like that, when they'd moved in a year ago, just before Andrew's seventh birthday, and he had enjoyed helping with them. Grandfather Kenney hadn't been able to help, because his eyes had been failing then and he'd still refused to wear glasses even for reading.

It had been hard to believe that the old man couldn't see. His eyes had still gleamed under the jutting, matted brows, still gripped you when you looked into them, while he was telling you the stories you never tired of hearing, stories mostly of ships and far countries and wild men and animals, many of whom Grandfather Kenney had been obliged to fight, for one reason and another.

Andrew couldn't remember that he'd really thought about his grandfather much, not when he'd been alive. He'd only started thinking about him consciously, and as much as he did now, after he'd died; and particularly on that day before the funeral.

They'd been in the drawing-room, the big room with the open fire-place and all those beams in the ceiling. Andrew wasn't allowed in it usually, except on special occasions; Susan Fowler kept it clean and neat, and they only used it when there were people in.

His mother, who was Grandfather Kenney's daughter, had been half crying all that day. The funeral, Andrew knew, was to be on the next day, and he'd asked her what time it was going to be and whether he'd have to wear his school clothes, and she'd looked horrified.

"Oh, no, Andrew! You don't want to be there."

"But I must!" Even to his own ears his voice had come in a high, thin squeak. The idea of not being allowed to go was terrible.

"No, Andrew. You'll stay here."

His mother had turned away, blowing her nose again, and he caught his father's hand. "Please, I must! If Grandfather was alive he'd want me to—I can't *not*!"

He just knew he had to. Not to go would be like passing his grandfather in the street and looking the other way.

John Fowler touched his son's head. "Your mother's right; a funeral's no place for a boy. Just a lot of grown-ups, and—well, you'll be better here, old chap."

*   *   *

Andrew drew the curtains apart carefully, taking care not to make a noise; they didn't like him getting up too early, and he wasn't sure of the time. Certainly there was no sound from anywhere else in the house.

For some reason or other it always pleased them to find him still asleep when one of them came in, in the mornings; sometimes, just to make them happy like that, he lay doggo with the sheet over his face and went through an act of waking up, sleepy.

He pulled off his pyjamas and dressed quickly in vest and pants, the school shorts and shirt and sweater and the grey stockings with dark blue tops. But he didn't bother with the tie, and he went along the passage past his parents' room, and down the stairs, on his stockinged feet. In the lobby between the kitchen and the back door he stepped into his gumboots; then he unlocked the outside door and went out into the sharp, damp morning air and shut the door quietly behind him.

The snowdrops and the aconites were over but the trees were still bare; only the weeping willows, four of them down in that lowest corner of the lawn above the stream, had a yellow-greenish sheen about them from the tips of tiny, half-formed buds. Crocuses were out, thick around the boles of the young fruit trees; but only mauve ones now; sparrows had picked the yellow flowers to shreds. He moved down across the lawn, which was getting tufty in the rougher places and would need to be cut before long; his boots, shiny black as wet seals, left clear, dark tracks in the lightly frosted grass. The ground was hard, but not rock-hard as it had been during most of the winter months.

The gate into the paddock was just below the timber garage that housed his father's business car and his mother's baby station-wagon. He was heading for the gate, intending to pause there long enough to enjoy the daydream he always had just there—the dream that a pony, *his* pony, grazing in the paddock, whinnied at him when it saw him there—when he remembered the guinea-pig. It had to be fed: and his parents objected less strongly to his creeping out of the house and mooching around at what they called 'the crack of dawn' if he did something useful at the same time. Andrew turned about and walked back towards the mellowed stone bulk of the house, treading carefully in the footprints he'd made in the stiff, wet grass.

When he'd filled the piebald rodent's tin bowl with the mixture of bran and corn, poured fresh milk into its bowl and given it a new carrot, he watched it for a minute or two, then came back down from its hutch on the higher bit of lawn, the flat part on the other side of the house, and fell in with the line of his own tracks again and went to the gate to think about the pony. There was a rib of frost along the top of the gate, so he didn't sit on it, for fear of messing up his school shorts, which experience had taught him could lead to trouble.

The pony would have been disappointed when he'd turned round short of the gate and gone away again; now it would whinny again and come right up to him, and he'd pet it and talk to it for a minute. Andrew did that now, just as if the animal was there on the other side of the gate while he stood on the lowest bar and leant over to fondle its ears. He told it quietly, knowing how a voice could carry on cold mornings, "I'll ride you when I get back from school." But another thought struck him: he could groom the pony *now*, before breakfast. He clambered over the gate and led the pony with his hand buried in its mane, down to the stable which backed against the garden hedge, just above the stream which ran below and past the garden willows and on down the slope of the valley floor, making the lower edge of this paddock; where it passed the next long straggle of hedgerow, that was the farthest corner of the Fowlers' land. From there on, and on the other side of the stream, was farmland. Over on that side of it fields rose steeply to a wooded crown of hill; cattle grazed there usually, but at this time the hillside was empty of everything but crows.

Andrew led the pony over the rough, thick grass of the paddock, avoiding the easier and more direct route which was a car-width track floored with brick rubble and cinders. The people who'd sold this place to the Fowlers had used the stable as an extra garage, and laid the track for that purpose. The stable still smelt of car—of petrol and fumes and rubber. Andrew closed his mind to that: filled his senses with a scent of horse and straw, the way a stable *ought* to smell.

It would be hard on a pony at first, this aroma of the garage; Andrew had mentioned that to Grandfather Kenney, one day soon after they'd moved in, when Andrew hadn't yet started school and on a day when Susan Fowler had seemed practically demented at all the difficulties she was meeting in her efforts to get the house straight; she'd been so busy and distracted that the old man and his grandson had sought refuge in the garden. They'd come down here to the stable-turned-garage to be turned, one day, back into a stable, and Andrew had mentioned the oily smell and how his pony wouldn't like it much; he'd asked

Grandfather Kenney if he knew of any quick way of getting rid of it.

The old man had looked around him slowly—he did everything slowly, by that time—and then, turning his deep, gleaming eyes down towards the boy, he'd chuckled and gestured round the stable with his stick.

"Any 'orse worth 'is keep 'll soon 'ave it smelling right. You leave that to '*im*, boy!"

Grandfather Kenney had shuffled over to the far side of the stable then, where there was a kind of window that had no glass in it but only a heavy wooden shutter hinged along its top edge. He'd leant his stick against the wall of the stable, and used both hands to push it open; the edges were festooned with cobwebs and compressed dirt, and the hinges groaned as if they hadn't been shifted in years.

The old man peered out through the opening, silhouetted against the surprising light that flooded in; his breath was noisy from the effort he'd exerted, and Andrew guessed that he was resting as much as looking out.

"There'll be a latch, most likely, boy, on the outside there, to 'old this open. Nip round and 'ave a look, eh?"

Between them they'd latched it open, and it had been open ever since, an aperture some four feet square—quite big enough for a horse to stick his head through—facing across the stream through lean brambles towards the rising slope of fields.

But the place still reeked of car.

*　　*　　*

"How many hours have you been up and tearing round?"

The boy looked up at his mother as if the question surprised him. She'd just about got the breakfast ready; Andrew's porridge was smelling like porridge and at any minute John Fowler would be rushing down to gulp up two soft-boiled eggs and two cups of coffee before he got his car out on to the road for London.

"How long? You mean—up?"

She nodded, lifting the saucepan of hot milk off the stove.

He scratched his knee. "Just long enough to feed the pig."

She glanced at him sharply, her eyebrows up. He added, "I was in the stable when you called me."

Her eyes hadn't left him.

He told her, "It stinks, still. You'd think that window—"

"It'll stink a lot more if you have your way and put some wretched pony in it."

He smiled; it was a pleasant thought. "That's what Grandfather Kenney says. Said."

"What?" His father shot into the kitchen and on to his stool at that end of the table in one swift, continuous movement. He had the top off the first egg as he asked, "*What* did your grandfather say?"

"That my pony'll make the stable smell better."

John Fowler laughed, reaching for the coffee. "Your pony, eh? Well, well. Sugar—thank you. I'll tell you something, Andrew. If you ever have a pony, you'll have to look after it, and that includes keeping its stable clean. Nobody else will."

"I know. I want to."

Susan Fowler smiled. "We'd never have guessed. Eat your porridge, Andrew." Thinking about the pony and looking at his father, he hadn't even seen it, right under his nose. She told him, "Remind me, I must give you the invitations to hand out when you get to school."

Andrew nodded. They'd written out the cards together, last evening. For his birthday party, a week from Saturday; he was asking most of the children in his class. He didn't much want a party, but he'd been to several of the others' and his mother had said he had to give one too, so as not to be rude. It was pretty staggering, the things you had to go through just not to be rude. He'd discussed that with his grandfather too, in some other, now remote, connexion, and Grandfather Kenney had told him that it was no damn good kicking against the pricks until you were big enough to win. So he hadn't told his mother that he'd rather kick half the children in school than have them along to tea. He'd just written his name in the space at the bottom of each card, where she'd told him to.

John Fowler finished his breakfast and collected his hat and coat and briefcase and came struggling back into the kitchen; he kissed his wife and told Andrew to behave himself at school. A minute later they heard the engine of his car roaring as he drove it up the short, steep drive into the lane. The sound faded quite suddenly, as it always did just when he rounded the corner; Andrew swallowed another mouthful of porridge and thought to himself that by now his father would be across the Speldhurst road and in the lane that wound by Poundsbridge: in ten minutes, about when it would be time to get ready for school, he'd be passing that enormous house at Penshurst. The one that belonged to Lord someone, who got a Victoria Cross in the First World War.

It occurred to Andrew that, to have got that, his Lordship would have to be very much the same sort of man that Grandfather Kenney had been.

II

H E DROVE carefully over the narrow high-backed bridge that
crossed the railway line, and turned left, and Bough Beech
fell behind; there was a light mist but it wasn't thick enough
for lights.

The fields were newly ploughed; the hop fields rigged and
tidy. Hedges had been trimmed, too, in most places, ready for the
spring growth; the countryside was in hand and full of promise.
He'd have liked, above all things, to have been a farmer.

Approaching Four Elms, he thought of Andrew at breakfast,
still quoting Kenney. The boy had always worshipped his grandfather, hung on his words and, in his absence, repeated his
stories and his slightest observation. John Fowler admitted to
himself a certain private unrest which he'd constantly tried to
hide; not jealousy exactly, but a feeling of his own inadequacy
as a father. When the old man had died, he'd thought that things
would change, that he and his son would draw closer. It hadn't
happened.

Compared to Grandfather Kenney, he had little to offer in the
way of glamour, boy-appeal. Kenney had fought in the trenches
in the first war; then he'd gone to sea, drifted about the world.
He'd mined gold in Australia, fought in a war in South America,
trapped animals in the Canadian northlands. Even if his yarns had
been exaggerated—a minor dispute becoming a fight to the
death, a half-caste Indian guide a war chieftain and blood-brother
—they'd all had something in them. Whereas John Fowler had
been just too young to see action in the second war, and was now
Sales Manager of a firm that made and sold pharmaceutical
products: pills, tonics, lotions, packaged to catch the eye.

He hadn't any stories that a boy would want to hear.

He'd taken the short cut through Chartwell; Westerham was just ahead. Then the long climb through thicker fog which thinned and cleared at Biggin Hill, thinning as the traffic thickened, the pace slowing as he nosed into the suburbs, Beckenham, Penge, rows of similar houses with similar cars backing out of their integral garages.

John Fowler wondered, as he pulled up behind a tight mass of other cars at a traffic light, how many of the drivers round him hated, as he did, being a part of it. Or thought about it at all? The lights changed, the cars ahead crept forward: a few turning at the intersection slowed the whole lot. The lights changed again to amber, red. He glanced to his right: a dark, Jewish-looking man at the wheel of a Mark X Jaguar grinned at him and spread his hands. Fowler grinned back, feeling suddenly a lift in nameless friendship. The man was old enough to have suffered, as a Jew, twenty years ago. Perhaps he had. Now he was the man next door—at least for the next seventeen seconds.

Without having thought about it, he'd wound the window down. He called across, "Why do we bother?"

The other man leant right across to his nearside window, still smiling, spread his hands again palms upward. He answered with his own question and the hands asked it too: "What else?"

The lights were green. Behind them, horns blared angrily.

He'd be at his desk in half an hour. And he was having lunch at a pub with Peter Anson, who'd started digging out his own escape route by breeding minks. He was making a success of it, so he'd said; and it had occurred to John Fowler that there'd be plenty of room for something like that in the paddock. Better than using it for a pony which nobody'd have time to look after . . .

*   *   *

He thought about Anson all afternoon and all the way home: well, most of the way. Driving was an automatic process; sometimes he got so lost in thought that, coming-to, there'd be a moment's almost frantic re-entry to the present, a struggle to recognise quickly enough where he was to get into the right traffic lane before the next turn.

Those minks were flourishing. In two years, starting from scratch and some book or other, Anson had broken even, covered his costs so that from now on every skin he sold was profit. Like John Fowler and a million others, he hated office work; unlike most of them, he'd started doing something about it.

Heading south through Keston on the Westerham road, John Fowler switched on his radio for the news bulletin. Cassius Clay, apparently, was having hysterics on the eve of his fight with Liston. (Who wouldn't?) The Foreign Secretary had suggested at Geneva that everyone should burn certain weapons and put observers in each other's countries. (The weapons were obsolete; observers were there already, classified as diplomats or spies.) A circus, moving out of its winter quarters to some place near the coast and passing through Southborough in Kent (*Southborough?*) had mislaid a lion; local residents were warned to keep children and pets indoors until someone shot it.

Steady drizzle all the way; the petrol man who filled his tank at Biggin Hill stared at him belligerently as if the customer was responsible for the weather.

Southborough. That was just north of Tunbridge Wells, a stone's throw east of Speldhurst. . . .

But now Westerham: and darkish now, up from side to head-lights. The days were lengthening, though; ten days ago it had been headlights all the way from London. It was the cloud, and drizzle. Over the A.25, and southwards again, and only half an hour to go for home. Friday, thank God: two days' peace ahead. But how did a circus lose a lion, for heaven's sake? And why should it be on the move this early in the year? For that matter, what lion in its right mind would leave a warm, dry cage for the wilds of an English February?

But it was mild enough. After that early frost, the rain had sent the mercury shooting up. At home, Susan would have turned off the central heating. He wondered if she'd heard that bulletin, or an earlier one. Andrew had better stay indoors until the beast was caught—or rather, shot, the man had said. Rather hard luck on it; it couldn't have known the penalty for escaping would be sudden death. Who'd do the shooting—Constable Williams? He had his hands full already, with summonses and fallen trees.

Penshurst: dark, winding lanes like tunnels flooded briefly, brightly by his headlights. Left fork at Poundsbridge; then up that hill and sharply down again to the right into a lane more like a drainpipe than a tunnel. Uphill again, winding, lights in cottage windows. It was ridiculous to think that a lion might lurk in one of those simple gardens.

*   *   *

Susan was at the stove, stirring something; as he pushed in and leant back against the door to shut it, she turned, and from the expression on her face he saw at once that she'd heard about the lion.

"Hi, darling. Everything all right? Where's Andrew?"

She pointed at the ceiling with a wooden spoon. "In his bath."

"Bit early, isn't it? Has he had his supper?"

She nodded. "I didn't want him to hang around outside this evening. So he started early."

John Fowler dropped his briefcase on the table, put his hat on top of it, began to unbutton his raincoat. He was waiting for her to tell him; he could see she was all ready to. Pointing at the long north window, she told him, "There's a man-eating tiger out there somewhere. Constable Williams has been rushing round on his bicycle, warning everyone. That's why I kept Andrew in."

He grinned. "In case he did it an injury?" He imitated her dramatically pointing finger: "It's not necessarily out *there*. It escaped at Southborough—four miles away by crow. And it's just as likely to have gone east as west."

"Four miles isn't far, John. Anyway, Williams is quite het up about it. You haven't kissed me."

He came round the table to put that right. "You haven't given me a chance. Jabbering away about this tiger—"

"Lion." It was Andrew, in pyjamas, bare-footed in the door-way. His father nodded.

"Right. As I was about to say, jabbering about a tiger which happens to be a lion. And nobody said anything about man-eating, did they?"

Andrew asked his mother, "Shall I go to bed now?"

"Cleaned your teeth?"

The boy nodded.

"All right then. Daddy'll be up in a minute to hear your prayers."

"Not you?"

"Both of us, then. Up you go!"

They heard his feet slip-slapping on the polished stairs. Later, when they'd tucked him in and come down again, Susan said, "I wish I hadn't told Andrew about this lion thing. He's so imaginative, he'll be having nightmares again."

"He's imaginative, all right. But you couldn't keep it secret. Everyone'll know, by now—including all the other kids at school. Gin and tonic?"

She sighed. "That sounds delicious." He went out to slice a lemon and get ice. When he was back and pouring the drinks, she asked him from behind the evening paper, "Weren't you lunching with that odd man Anson today?"

He gave her the drink. "We had a snack in a pub. What's so odd about him?"

Susan laughed. "I'll admit his wife's odder . . . It's on that shelf."

"Oh. Thanks." It was his tobacco that he'd been groping for. She asked him, "Did he tell you about his minks?"

"He certainly did. That's what I wanted to see him about." He paused, looking at her. "I thought we might do the same thing here."

"I need another drink."

"All right." He took her glass. "Peter's got rows and rows of cages now. From now on, it's all profit. Well, damn it—why shouldn't we do that?"

"It wouldn't be we, darling. It'd be you. And you're in London all day."

"I'd see to them in the evenings, when I get home. Feed them, I mean. Collect the stuff once a week, mix it up and keep it in a special fridge—in the old garage down there."

"The old garage." She was taking it seriously now. "You mean the stable? Where Andrew'll have his pony one of these days? Cages in the paddock?"

He nodded.

"And the pony?"

"There isn't any pony! Andrew's too young yet. All that space—don't you see, we could make something of it? Use it constructively: something we could do ourselves, *for* ourselves."

They looked at each other; she showed no trace of his own enthusiasm. He reached for the matches and said quietly, "You don't see, do you?"

She frowned. "What am I supposed to see, John?"

"That like everyone else I'm trapped into this commuting thing. A mass of us rushing to and fro as if we were driven by Martians with whips. Like animals in circuses—jumping through hoops and standing on tubs, then back to the straw until it's time for the next ludicrous, humiliating performance. D'you see?"

"Of course . . . I'd say you were pitching it a bit strong."

She was silent for a minute, while he sipped his gin.

"It can't be all that simple, can it? Snags in it—"

"Of course there'll be snags. But we won't be relying on it for a living. I'll be working while we build it up."

She took his hand. "I can't stop you, if you really want it. But, darling, don't rush into it right away. I mean, think about it."

"I've thought about it for months. But I won't be starting on the cages this week-end, if that's what you mean. . . . D'you think I'm being selfish?"

"No." She looked at him. "No, I don't think that at all."

"But you'd rather use that field and the stable for a pony for Andrew, wouldn't you?"

She nodded. "Yes, I would. And, John, don't tell Andrew about this yet. He's still missing his grandfather: in the last few days he's got worse—sort of brooding. I was going to talk to you about it; a pony might have taken him out of his daydreams."

"But so might the minks. He'd get a lot of fun out of them; help with them, if he wanted to. And what's more, if it worked out, we could really afford things like ponies. And . . ."

"And what?"

He'd been about to say, 'And a proper dress allowance for you.' It had been one of the things in his mind for a long time. He didn't spend nearly enough on her. But he didn't mention it now because he didn't want it to sound like bribery.

*   *   *

The night was hot: at least, it was in Andrew's room. Outside it was mild enough; the rain had finished, leaving the air clear and the temperature high for this time of year. But inside, not trusting any such indications, the Fowlers had left the heating on—at its lowest setting—just in case things changed and they woke to normal February temperatures.

Andrew's bed was a furnace: tossing about in half-sleep, he almost glowed with heat. Perhaps the fact that he was never still had something to do with it. He was asleep, but part of him was in touch with the waking world, struggling to resist the fantasies, flash-glimpses of faces that grinned and scowled and shouted to tell him things, meaningless things but still disturbing, even maddening in their remoteness, which rushed through his mind like planned, inflicted torments on a soul in hell. There was some kind of denial in it all, a negative quality that hovered on the brink of terror: when he woke suddenly to the moonlit room his reaction was of enormous relief, flooding peace and reassurance, thankfulness in escape.

He lay on his back, sweating, staring wide-eyed at the moonlight. He wondered if he'd called out in his sleep; if he had, his mother would be along at any moment. That happened sometimes, waking both of them; he never knew why he'd called, and he'd satisfy her usually by saying he wanted a drink of water.

It was easier to do that than to meet the questions he couldn't answer. Well, this time it was all right; she'd have been here by now.

He threw back the bed-clothes; he did that, in the first place, because of the heat, but as soon as he'd done it it seemed as if it was really the first step in a whole series as he scrambled right out of the sweat-damp bed and let the moonlight draw him to the window.

His room had only this one window in it, and it looked across the falling slope of the garden and the stream, which was invisible from here but marked by the line of tall, thin hedge. Beyond that the fields rose clearly, cleanly in the moonlight, pale silver ribbed with black hedgerows and their pools of shadow, to the hill's top with its spreading stain of woodland. Almost at the top of the first field, the big one, Andrew saw the lion.

It was the size of a calf, only its head and shoulders were infinitely more powerful: it tapered away to almost nothing at the flanks. It was well out into the field, walking slowly, deliberately from left to right—which meant, from south to north—as if it had a definite purpose and objective, in the course of which it was crossing that field from one dark hedgerow to the other. There was no kind of haste in that purpose, no urgency; only a sureness, an immense dignity of slow, powerful movement.

Andrew stood like a statue at the window, watching the lion. He was not surprised, and certainly not alarmed. Elated would be a better word to describe his state of mind. And—this was what kept the elation quiet in him—quite extraordinarily impressed. He had not expected anything one half so wonderful.

But when the lion was well out into the centre of the field, Andrew realised that the glass of the window in front of him was misty from the breath which he'd thought he'd been holding. The scene out there was blurred. He unlatched the window at the bottom and pushed it open.

Probably the swinging glass of the window caught and reflected a flash of moonlight back into the field. That explanation never occurred to Andrew. All he knew was that he opened the window to see the lion more clearly, and the lion stopped absolutely dead and swung its enormous head and stared straight at him. What with the height of the house, the downward slope of the garden and the upward slope of the field, Andrew and the lion were at just about the same level.

Moonlight lit the smouldering amber of its eyes; moonlight dappled its flanks and showed in contrast the mane like an ink-dark shawl over its neck and shoulders.

It turned then, swiftly, so that he hardly saw the movement; but now all he could see was the great head and the eyes that burned like molten iron. Watching it, he clutched the window sill, leaned forward so that his head was right through the window in the cool, night air. He was willing it, now, to come downhill, closer, to cross the stream; he wanted it close enough to touch.

But when it moved, and he caught his breath in sudden, new excitement, it was to turn away from him. As if it had lost interest, or had seen enough. Or perhaps it had remembered its original purpose and destination. It swung away, and there was no longer any glow of eyes; just its shape and movement as it resumed that graceful but at the same time ponderous crossing of the field. Andrew watched the distance lessening between the lion and the dark shadowed depths of the other hedgerow, which was deeper still because of the trees that lined it on its other side; once it got there it would be lost to him, and he longed to call out, to implore it to stay and to look back at him again as it had been doing.

But he didn't call out. That would have woken people and brought his mother running, and that would have been to betray the lion, which was unthinkable.

If he'd thought of moving the window again to catch the moon, perhaps it might have brought the lion back. But Andrew didn't know about that, and the lion stalked on, out of the moonlight and his sight. Andrew stayed at the window for a long time in case it turned at the hedge or rested in the shadows and then came back; but he didn't really expect it to. It had so obviously known where it was and where it was going.

It had even known which window to look at.

Only when he left the window and crawled back into the chaos of his bed, which was cool now but still damp, did the boy realise that his face was all running wet. He hadn't even known that he'd been crying.

III

"**B**UGGERED if I know. And shut your perishin' trap, will you, mate?"

Corporal Lanning of No. 2 Section was answering a civil but unlawful question from Private 'Poet' Frith. Like all the others in B Company, Frith and the rest of the section were anxious to know why they'd been held back while the rest of the East Loamshires had boarded their transport and left for the airfield on schedule, more than an hour ago. But only Frith would have asked the question from the ranks, loudly and within earshot of Sergeant Crown, whose bite—particularly in the early hours of the morning—was invariably worse than his bark.

"And keep it shut," gritted 'Garbage' Higgins out of the side of his mouth. As he spoke he saw that sergeants and corporals were falling out. One of the HQ Platoon's runners had just doubled up to Sergeant Crown, and said something, and Crown had called his minions out. The whole lot of them, and the NCOs from the other platoons too, were trotting over towards a group outside the Company CO's office.

Crowborough, Sussex, the site of this camp, was still asleep under drifting mist and opaque, grey skies. The Battalion had stood-to at dawn; they'd been ready for the move for several days. The new General out in Cyprus, Frith had told the rest of the section confidentially, had 'asked for them special'. They'd been waiting, the Battalion of more than five hundred men, for the aircraft to get back from their shuttle-service to East Africa. Only B Company remained now, drawn up in platoons and sections on the wet, black tarmac. Their Armoured Personnel Vehicles were waiting too, loaded and fuelled, on the other side of the long row of huts.

Frith began to sing quietly under his breath,

> "Makarios, Makarios, 'ere we come!
> Shove your beaver—"

"Ah, shut it, mate!" That was Meadows, on his left. No. 2 Section was always being picked on, and the reason for it was nearly always Frith. It wasn't that they minded his poetry; they were used to that. Even the Company CO, Major Willesley, had been reported to have a keen appreciation of it, having the choicer verses retailed to him via the NCOs of HQ Platoon. But the sergeants and corporals were on their way back, and No. 2 Section's eyes were fixed on Lanning as he changed smartly from the double to a stiff military strut and halted to their front with the kind of crash the army liked.

"Prop'ly at ease!"

They stiffened.

"'Ear this then. The Company will not leave for Cyprus with the remainder of the Battalion. Not until further notice."

"Why the 'ell not, Corp?" That was Frith, of course.

"Silence in the ranks! Private Frith, when you falls out, report to me!" The corporal glared furiously at the poet.

"The rest of you'll return to your 'uts and await further orders. Immediate readiness!" His voice fell to almost normal tones; No. 2 Section heard the muted roars of other sections' NCOs handing out the same guff. Lanning told them, "In confidence and for your dirty ear 'oles only, I'll let you in on a secret. You're goin' on a lion 'unt."

No. 2 Section laughed happily. They were always ready for a joke.

*   *   *

"Not a sound from Andrew. He must be still asleep!" Susan said it, at the dressing-table. John Fowler smiled as he laced his shoes. For their son to be still asleep at half-past eight would be a record indeed.

A thought struck Susan: it froze her, the hair-brush poised in mid-air.

"You did tell him he wasn't to go outside this morning?" She jerked round to face her husband. "John?"

"Well—" he glanced up, frowning. "Not specifically. But he knows, he wouldn't have—"

She'd gone, like a gust of wind, out of the room and down the passage. He stood up, stretched, yawned, crossed over to the dressing-table where she'd been sitting, and stooped down to straighten his tie. He heard Susan talking to Andrew then, in the boy's room; he grinned at himself in the mirror, shaking his head and sharing amusement with his own reflection.

No wonder so many small boys thought their mothers were slightly potty.

"Oh, thank—you *are* here!" she'd exclaimed, finding him in his room. Then, as he turned from the window to greet her, she saw that he looked pale as well as surprised at her explosive entry. "Andrew, are you feeling all right?"

He was dressed and he'd brushed his hair, which in itself was unusual, and he'd been standing at the window of his room, his elbows on its sill, gazing out at the fields. She bent to kiss his forehead; straightening, with one hand resting lightly on his shoulder, she looked out to see what could have been holding his silent, rapt attention. But the fields were empty; they looked exactly as they had the day before. And his forehead had felt hot and dampish to her lips.

"Are you all right, Andrew?"

He nodded. "Yes, thank you."

His flat, polite tone alarmed her. She said quickly, "All the same, I'm going to take your temperature." He shook his head; she added firmly, "Just in case."

"I'm all right, really. It's only that I usually go out and you didn't want me to."

"Did you sleep all right?"

His eyes flickered to the window. "Yes, thank you." She told him cheerfully, wanting to buck him up, "It'll only be until they shoot that lion, and they're bound to find it soon. And today it doesn't matter, because we're going to Brighton, remember?"

His eyes were on hers and they looked frightened. "They

wouldn't shoot it, would they?" He'd moved away from her, back to the window; he was staring out at the fields, as he had been when she'd burst into the room. She moved up beside him and put her arm back round his shoulders: she could feel that he was trembling.

"Why, it's a danger to everyone. Lions are savage—you know that. Nobody's safe until they find it. And animals—sheep, chickens, even cows, I suppose—it'll get hungry and it'll kill whatever it finds. You can see that, can't you?"

"It wouldn't hurt anyone." His tone was obstinate. "They've no right to shoot it when it isn't doing any harm. That's wrong! Why don't they leave it alone? Or they could feed it—"

"Lions take a lot of feeding, old chap." John Fowler had come into the room behind them. "And they're carnivores. That means they eat meat. In the circus he'd have a great hunk of raw stuff every day. Out in the country he'll have to kill to get anything —as your mother said."

"Circus?" Andrew turned quickly. "Is that where they say he's come from?"

"Yes. It got out of one of those wagon things, a cage on wheels. You know."

Something like contempt flickered in the boy's eyes. "I suppose they've got to say something like that."

His parents glanced at each other. John Fowler forced a laugh. "I don't know what you mean by that, Andrew. Anyway, there's nothing we can do about it and nothing for us to worry about." He turned to Susan. "How about breakfast?"

"I'll go down and start. Will you take Andrew's temperature, please? He's—off-colour, whatever he says." As she went down the passage she called back, "It's in the bathroom cupboard."

"H'm. Well, come on, old lad. We'll perform this operation in the bathroom." Andrew, following him along the passage, said, "I'm perfectly all right, I said I was."

"Good. Mothers worry, though. Just as well, sometimes." He pointed at the stool. "Sit." Fiddling among the bottles he found the thermometer, shook it down and pushed it into the boy's mouth. "Now hold it still under your tongue. I'll be back in a moment." Andrew grunted. When John Fowler came back, his son had the glass tube in his hand, examining it closely.

"It's normal, all right."

"I told you to keep it in, Andrew."

"I know. But I had to sneeze and it would have broken. Anyway, it's normal. Look."

It was. John Fowler sighed. All this, and Brighton too. Susan wanted to do some shopping there, and he was to take Andrew round the aquarium and on the pier.

"Well, all right. But you'd better eat a particularly large breakfast, just to make your mother happy. Otherwise she's bound to take it again. Eh?"

When he got downstairs himself, a few minutes later, Andrew wasn't in the kitchen. Susan asked him, "Did you take it?"

"Normal. There's nothing wrong with him that fresh air won't cure." He kissed her. "Nothing to worry about. For some reason he's upset about that bloody lion."

"That's just why I didn't want to tell him about it! His imagination—I really must talk to the doctor about him."

He shook his head. "Try not to worry so much; he'll grow out of it. If we fuss it'll aggravate it. . . . Where is he, anyway?"

He found him in the study, standing against the window. It was a high one and the boy's chin only just topped the polished wooden sill. Outside this window was the place where they always fed the birds with scraps and crusts; there was a tangled quince tree a dozen feet from the wall, its lower branches white with droppings. Standing behind his son, John Fowler watched a bullfinch hopping along one of the top boughs, methodically pecking out the hearts of new buds so small that they were invisible from this distance.

But suddenly he realised that Andrew wasn't watching the bird; he was staring up past the tree, his eyes on the empty fields.

"Are you—er—expecting to see the lion up there?"

Andrew jumped as if something had bitten him. He stammered, "Up—up where?"

John Fowler pointed. "Up in that field, eh? You think that's where he's like to show up? Good lion country?"

"No!" The boy was scarlet. "I was just—well, *looking*."

"You haven't by any chance seen anything up there, have you?"

"*Seen* anything? Why should I? I was just *looking*, it could be there, there aren't any houses or anything." His father was watching him curiously as his voice petered out in too shrill innocence. Such a violent reaction, to a question that had been half a leg-pull . . .

After they'd had breakfast John Fowler got his shotgun out of its case and assembled it; he slipped a couple of No. 5 cartridges into his pocket and went quietly out of the side door. Bird-shot wouldn't be much use on a lion, if he did meet one; but it might scare it off, which would be a lot better than nothing, and anyway it gave him a feeling of protection. It was easy enough to laugh about strayed lions when you were safely indoors; out here the comfort of the gun's weight under his arm was a welcome thing. Before he went any farther he pushed the cartridges into the breech.

Rounding the corner of the greenhouse and expecting to see nothing but empty garden, he started and caught his breath at the sight of a human figure. Then, ashamed of his taut nerves, he relaxed and called "Good morning!"

"Mornin', sir." Dingett, the gardener, only came on Saturdays. Fowler had forgotten that it was his day. The old man, who came from Suffolk and still sounded like it, was rough-digging the potato bed.

"You're not worried about this lion, then?"

"Ah, no, sir." Dingett stopped work and planted his fork viciously in the hard black earth. "'E won't want to eat oi, not 'less 'e's barmy." He smiled, baring pink gums and National Health Service teeth. "If 'e do come by, oi'll give 'm a good clout wi' me fork 'ere." Shrewd blue eyes rested on the 12-bore under his employer's arm. "You'm ready for 'm, then."

John Fowler was embarrassed. The old man's implication seemed to be that he was making a lot of fuss about nothing. He said, "We'll be out most of the day. I'll leave this in the greenhouse, in case you want it."

Dingett just grinned again, and went on digging.

John Fowler prowled slowly round the garden, looking into all the hedgerows and bushes, keeping an eye on the neighbouring fields. Well, it was probably a waste of time, the lion a dozen miles away; still you never knew, and a man had his responsibilities. Even if he didn't have much else, he had those. He thought of the friendly Jew in that long, sleek car: *What else?*

At the gate to the paddock he paused, and let his eyes rove around the hedgerows. He wouldn't bother, he told himself, to walk round the little field. Then it struck him that if he was doing this at all, not to do it thoroughly was to make the whole thing pointless. He was being lazy: or—he thought of Dingett's quiet, countryman's smile—cowardly? Scared, calling it off now to avoid going round the hidden corner and along that stream's edge, that deep bank where if a lion was hiding now he wouldn't see it until he was almost on top of it?

Trying to analyse his own weakness he followed the line of the stream with his eyes from the far corner of the paddock along the straggly budding hedge to the stable which hid this nearer bottom corner from his view.

That stable door was open.

But nothing new in that. It always was. All the same, it was shelter, that stable or garage or whatever it was or was going to be; a deserted spot, a corner no one passed or used. A dim place as likely as any within a radius of miles.

Or behind it, in the corner of two hedges and the stream's bank falling steeply, all out of sight. If he was looking for anything, for any animal, even for a child playing hide and seek, wouldn't that be about the only likely place, the obvious one to check?

John Fowler pushed the gate open with some difficulty; it needed all his strength just to open it far enough for him to squeeze through. He thought, I must see to that: needs rehanging. He left the gap open behind him, paused while he glanced down at the gun; his thumb moved, without his really having told it to, and eased the safety-catch forward. He thought,

If I'd asked Dingett to look around in that corner, in the stable, he'd have strolled down humming, empty-handed.

Well, Dingett has no imagination. I have. That's where young Andrew gets it from.

Did the boy see something, up on the hill, earlier this morning? While he was dressing? If he'd had to make a bet on it, at that moment John Fowler would have answered yes. It didn't make for comfort. His hands were sweating and the cinders crunched under his feet. He stepped off the track on to the grass, and moved off at an angle to the cinders, to skirt the stable with its open door and check behind it first. He'd be able to see behind it, into that hidden corner of the paddock, without going really close to the stable itself. He couldn't hear his own footsteps now, the grass was soft and thick. All he could hear was his own breathing.

Nothing behind the shed, except brambles and old dead nettles. He went on down to the bottom hedge, above the fall to the stream. Nothing there either; he could see along the stream to his left all along to the corner, and to his right for ten or fifteen yards. Well, forget the rest of that: now the stable.

He was holding the gun clear in front of him now, his left hand under the barrels and his right on the narrow of the stock. Just as if he was walking-up partridges. He felt damp all over, as hot as if he was in one of the first rooms of a Turkish bath; the grass was still patched white, here and there, with frost.

The side of the stable brushed his right elbow and he pulled that arm in closer and stepped wider. There wasn't any sound from inside it. Then he was at the corner, the open doorway a dark crack growing broader as he took the next step and slewed his body round to face it squarely; and suddenly it was over, he was in the doorway, hit by a wave of relief that was almost painful in its intensity; he could see into every corner of the stable, and the place was empty. Just as it always had been. Empty, dark, smelling of oil and rubber.

John Fowler leant against the inside of the doorpost and his thumb pulled the gun's safety-catch back to 'safe'. He would have laughed with relief except that he felt a kind of shame. There wasn't any doubt in his mind now about where Andrew got his fierce imagination from. They should both of them be more like Dingett.

On the way back to the house it was going to be difficult to meet that old man's flinty eyes. He would have liked to rest here until he'd cooled off and brought his breathing under proper control. But if he stayed too long, Susan would miss him and start calling.

Before he left the stable, he shut the door and bolted it. At least he wouldn't have to go through all that again.

*   *   *

Corporal Lanning snapped his notebook shut and glanced round at them. "That's about the lot, then. Move off in 'alf an hour. Any more daft questions before I tear myself away?"

The men of No. 2 Section—of the whole Company, for that matter—were now aware that the lion-hunt story was not a joke at all, but the true reason for their remaining in half-frozen England while the rest of the Battalion was on its way to the blue skies and warmth of Cyprus. They'd been looking forward to that sunshine, and to the feel of active service—even if that did amount to nothing much more than being shot at with live ammunition. Basically, it was the chance of service abroad, of doing real soldiers' jobs instead of training courses and parades, that they'd been looking forward to; a man didn't say such a thing, because if he did he'd almost certainly be laughed at, but they knew that their army was doing a job of international importance and they'd liked the idea of having a hand in that.

Frith and Meadows had translated their own disappointment into simpler and more personal worries. Their girl-friends, for instance, were expecting to have letters from the Trouble Spot, perhaps even to see their men on the TV news programmes, tanned heroes grinning across sunlit streets. There'd be a certain loss of face, when the girls learnt that their soldier lovers were patrolling nothing more exotic than the lanes of the Kent and Sussex border.

Lanning had retailed to them the gist of what he'd absorbed

and noted down at a briefing which the Company Commander had organised for the benefit of officers and NCOs. He'd sent a subaltern to rout the local Public Librarian out of his bed, in search of facts and figures.

"This 'ere lion," Corporal Lanning had told his men, referring constantly to the notebook in his hand, "is a full-grown male specimen. It will be approximately nine foot long and forty inches 'igh at the shoulder."

He'd paused then, to decipher his rapid, ball-point notes. 'Garbage' Higgins muttered, taking the whole thing badly, "They'll be at twenty thousand feet, by now. Over the bloody Alps, I shouldn't wonder."

Lanning switched his glare on. It faded as he looked down, frowning, at the notebook.

"The lion's general colouring is tawny, or golden, with dark or black 'air—known as the mane—on its neck. When merged into its surroundings—or, in plain language, camouflaged like— experienced 'unters 'ave found it useful to keep their eyes skinned for the black markings which are to be found on the animal's ears."

He glanced round at the puzzled but mostly interested faces. "They stand out, see, when the rest don't . . . Now, mark this. The lion, when angry, lays back its ears and adopts a snarling expression. It also lashes its tail from side to side." Corporal Lanning glanced up from his notes. "See? If you come across this lion and it wags its tail at you, that don't mean it's glad to see you. You don't *pat* it, you *shoots* it. See?"

They nodded at him. He went on quickly, holding up his free hand to keep their attention, "Regarding the animal's tail, 'owever: if that tail goes out rigid be'hind it and proceeds to jerk up vertical two or three times, that is the signal that it is about to launch an immediate attack."

"What's the drill then, Corp?"

Lanning stared gloomily at Frith, who had raised his hand as he asked the question. "If by that time you 'aven't clobbered 'im, Frith, I reckon you'll find the answer bloody quick."

*   *   *

There were sleet storms on the road south to Brighton, and a long traffic hold-up at Uckfield, so that the Fowlers got down to the sea later than they'd planned. It was dry in Brighton, but the wind was cold and strong; they'd brought a picnic lunch with them, and ate it sitting in the car, parked by the sea front. Then Susan Fowler went off on her shopping expedition, and as she'd said practically nothing about it Andrew felt pretty sure it had something to do with his birthday, which was now only six days ahead. He was interested, of course, in what they planned to give him, and made one or two mental guesses, but he wasn't really excited about it as he always had been at such times before. He made a half-hearted attempt to raise the subject with his father, when the two of them set off down the slope to the shingled beach; when the attempt was blocked he let it go, in fact forgot all about it at once.

Andrew threw stones into the grey sea for a bit, while his father watched him and wandered about inspecting the boats that were drawn up at the top of the shingle; but he soon got tired of stone-throwing, and John Fowler, who wasn't much absorbed in it either and in fact was uncomfortable and bored standing around in the cold wind, readily agreed to going straight along to the aquarium, which would at least be warm.

The attendant seemed surprised and glad to see them, and when they got inside, between the rows of great glass tanks, they found they had the place entirely to themselves. They moved from tank to tank, reading the labels and staring at the fish, and the fish stared back at them with much the same air of gloomy dis-interest. Andrew liked the turtles, and he spent quite a long time watching the seals, but his mind wasn't really on any of it. John Fowler kept the pace down as much as he could, pausing to express interest even in fish that looked quite dead and never moved; it was pleasantly warm in the aquarium, and he knew that Susan would be in no rush over her shopping.

When they'd been all round, he asked his son if he wouldn't like to go back for another look—at the turtles, for instance—but Andrew shook his head.

John Fowler sighed. "Well: like to go on the pier?"

"No, thanks. Not unless you would."

They went out, and in the entrance hall the attendant looked at them sadly as if they were the last people he could hope to see for at least another month. They went and sat in the car, John Fowler smoking his pipe and Andrew staring out of the window at shivering passers-by, until Susan Fowler appeared half an hour later with her arms full of parcels.

They got home in time for tea, and the light was already fading; it looked as if there might be more snow coming. At the Langton crossroads there were two army transports parked, and quite a lot of soldiers standing round them, stamping their feet and blowing out cigarette smoke; John Fowler and his wife glanced at each other when they'd passed the trucks and turned the corner, but neither of them said anything and Andrew had no idea what the soldiers could be there for.

IV

M RS HAILEY came from Rusthall and she 'did' for the Reginalds, who had one of those converted cottages up at Farnham. They were retired people and she liked them; she wouldn't have been going there for the best part of ten years if she didn't. She was a widow, and the late Mr Hailey hadn't left her nothing; she could have got by without ever doing another stroke, but if you stopped work when you were still fit for it, and had no better way to fill the days, you rotted.

She didn't live quite alone: she had old Blue. A Rough Terrier, she called him, and it wasn't a bad description. He was rough, and he was more terrier than anything else. She'd never pretended that he was something to show at Cruft's. She brought him to work at Farnham, of course; the Reginalds were very fond of him. She always walked to work, taking the short cut across the fields, and since she was by nature an early riser she made a habit of getting to the Reginalds so early that she'd have the downstairs all clean and tidy before the couple upstairs were ready to come down for their breakfast. Mrs Hailey worked to the clock; the late Mr Hailey had liked that, having things punctual and when he expected them and not getting taken by surprise, and she'd acquired the habit.

She always finished her work by midday, and that left her the afternoons to herself, and usually she'd take Blue for a walk unless there was something else she had to do. He got plenty of exercise, what with this walk across the fields at dawn and larking round the Reginalds' garden all morning and the walk back at noon. Now, when it was still darkish, she had him on the lead. If Blue had a fault, it was that he wouldn't always come when she called him, particularly out in these fields where sometimes he'd smell a rabbit, or imagine that he did. Mrs Hailey didn't much mind waiting around for him to come back in broad daylight, so long as it wasn't raining; but in the dark she didn't like it, and that was her reason for keeping him on the lead.

He was pretending, now, that he could smell something. It was a ruse, an attempt to fool her into letting him off. Well, it would take a lot more cunning than Blue could muster to fool Mrs Hailey. He ought to know that, by now; he'd tried it often enough.

"Come along, Bluey! Silly boy! Come along, now!"

But he went on pulling and snuffling towards that dark tangle of trees and rough stuff. She jerked quite hard at his lead and told him sharply, "Blue, will you *behave* yourself!"

He was really putting on an act, this morning. He was snarling viciously now, leaping out again and again against the pull of the lead so that once or twice it jerked him right off his scrabbling feet. He sounded as if he was strangling as much as snarling.

Perhaps there *was* a rabbit there. Or a pheasant or something. Well, Blue wasn't going to chase after it, that was certain. If she let him off the lead now she knew perfectly well he'd be out of sight in two split seconds, and by the time he condescended to return it would be daylight and she'd be late getting to the Reginalds.

But, really, Blue was like a mad thing! If he wasn't throwing a fit she didn't know what he *was* doing; Mrs Hailey had never seen him quite like this before. Well, she thought, I can't drag him all the way, he really will strangle himself—or break his neck. She'd no idea he was so strong; if the lead were to break, why—she thought, I'll pick him up, that's what I'll do! Pick him up and carry him, at least until we're past that patch of rough stuff.

Stooping, she pulled the dog in closer, to get hold of him by his collar. She leaned forward, towards him, and looped the lead around her left wrist to make sure he didn't catch her off balance and jerk it clean away. Then she reached out with her right hand to grab his collar.

Just as her hand was closing on the collar, Blue whipped round and bit her. She was so shocked and taken by surprise that for a moment she couldn't believe it had happened; the two smaller fingers and the outside of that hand flamed with pain and she staggered upright, shocked half to death.

She had dropped the lead, and Blue had leapt away towards that undergrowth around the saplings that grew out from the hedge. She stood holding her hand out away from her coat so as not to get the blood all over her; her mouth was open still in shocked amazement and the pain was flaring up her arm; she cried out, "Blue, you *bit* me!"

If Mrs Reginald had whipped round and bitten her in the hand, she could hardly have been more astounded.

Then she saw her dog leaping at that mass of shadow; and she saw the shadow rise to meet him. The lion growled: not loud, not ear-splitting like Blue's single, anguished yelp, but deep, blood-curdling, thick with menace.

Mrs. Hailey tried to scream, but she couldn't, she tried to but the air gagged in her throat and no sound came out. The only sounds she heard were the hard, sharp thud of the lion's paw as it knocked Blue flat on the ground, and the scrunch of Blue's skull as the lion's teeth closed on it.

*   *   *

The wind came up with daylight, from the east, biting cold in the steel February dawn, but down here in the valley where the lane ran it was deceptively gentle, its force deflected by the tops and shoulders of the hills. In their shadows the frost lay thick and white as snow. Elm, beech and birch along the hill-crests swayed to the wind, but down here they were still, their bare branches gaunt like the spars of anchored ships against the sky, and from the oaks on the high side of the lane an enormous congregation of rooks cawed and shifted restlessly, drifting down in noisy squadrons to patch the sheltered folds of grassland. Andrew Fowler woke with their raucous voices in his ears; closer still, starlings scratched and bickered in the eaves above his window.

He lay still, feeling the cold outside the bed-clothes, hearing the birds but not listening to them; remembering his dream.

He'd dreamt of waking, as he had woken on the night before, and of being drawn to the window where he stood and looked out at the moonlit fields; just where last night he'd seen the lion stalking in the moonlight, now he dreamt that he saw Grandfather Kenney. Alone on the bright and shadowed hillside the old man had come walking slowly, using his stick a great deal, as indeed he had during those last months before his legs had failed him altogether; he came slowly, purposefully out across that field, just where the lion had walked, and Andrew opened the bedroom window to see more clearly and also because he wanted to call out to his grandfather and to hear the old man answer him. When he'd opened the window, Grandfather Kenney had stopped, and turned, leaning heavily on that old stick and staring straight at him.

Then, when Andrew had tried to call out to him, he'd found he couldn't. He tried to wave; but his arms wouldn't obey him any more than his voice would. He struggled, fighting the terrifying inertia of drugged muscles, stifled breath, worried into a kind of panic that the old man would go on across the field without the passage of a word between them, dreading that Grandfather Kenney should think he'd just stood there watching him out on that frozen hillside and not said a word or raised a hand in greeting.

Struggling hadn't done any good, and the thing he dreaded happened. Grandfather Kenney got tired of waiting. With that strange, old-man's resignation he turned away, and plodded on, slowly and steadily across the field from left to right, his stick stabbing heavily into frozen turf, until like the lion on the night before he'd vanished into the shadows on the far side of the field.

That awful feeling of his own helplessness and of the sadness in the old man's face filled Andrew's mind as he lay in bed, awake now and remembering the dream. He knew it had been a dream, not real as the lion's appearance had been, and there was a certain comfort in that, if he could get at it. But just thinking about it, and of how it would have seemed to his grandfather if it *had* been real, still made him hot with shame. He realised, now that it was getting light and he was awake, that if in fact his grandfather had been up there on the hill he wouldn't have been able to see his face so clearly or recognise that loneliness in his eyes; but in spite of convincing himself over and over again that it had been only a dream, just knowing that he'd dreamt it made him sad.

One of the reasons Andrew never much liked going to bed in the evenings was that he so often had bad dreams. This one was far worse than the usual run of them, because it lingered in his mind instead of vanishing under the flood of relief which usually came with waking. He had to keep telling himself, still, that it hadn't happened. Andrew stared at the window, and listened. The cawing of the rooks, and those starlings scrabbling overhead: the faint smell of old timber and new paint: the house's inner silence: this was an ordinary morning—a Sunday morning, he remembered. That meant his father would be at home all day, that the three of them would be going to church, and that breakfast would be later than usual.

Judging by the light, Andrew reckoned that he had about two hours to wait for breakfast. Two hours which normally he'd spend outside in the garden, messing around with this and that, climbing in the big apple tree. It was good for climbing. And there was the paddock, and the stable, where he could think about his pony.

But today he couldn't do any of those things, because he wasn't allowed to go outside. His mother had told him that when he woke up he was to stay in bed and go straight back to sleep. He hadn't argued about that; it was one of his parents' blind spots, they simply couldn't understand that when you were wide awake you couldn't just decide to go to sleep, when you'd been asleep all night and weren't in the slightest tired any more.

He climbed out of bed and lay on the floor and leafed through some of his books. But the ones he liked he already knew by heart; he knew, before he turned each page, what the picture was on the other side of it; if it didn't have a picture he knew all the words. He could say them with his eyes shut, just about.

Andrew got out the magic lantern they'd given him last Christmas, and the strips of slides that showed, in four pictures each, the adventures of Lord Nelson and Jesse James and Popeye, Donald Duck, William Tell, Dick Turpin. He got right under his bed, to shine the pictures on the wall where it was dark. But the battery was low; Nelson looked very much like Turpin, except for Turpin's horse, which in the last slide lay dead, after galloping to York. Wherever that was. Nelson lay dead too.

Andrew switched off the projector and slid out from under the bed and began to get himself dressed. He didn't think much about dressing or whether he should; it was chiefly that he couldn't think of anything else to do. Then when he was dressed there wasn't much that he could do except go downstairs. He crept down, carrying his shoes in his hand. There was no sound from his parents' room as he passed it.

Downstairs the curtains were still across the windows and all the rooms were dark. Andrew went into the study, taking great care not to bump into anything; he went to the window and reached up to draw the curtains back, very slowly and gently so as not to make any noise. Then he looked out at the garden in its early, misty light; the lawn was frosted white and he wished that he could walk across it to leave his tracks looping around. The fun was, after that, to come in and go upstairs so that you could look down and see exactly where you'd been.

Just outside this study window the birds were in the quince tree, waiting for their breakfast of scraps. All the regulars: hunched sparrows, shiny starlings, a robin, a pair of hedge-sparrows. Several blue-tits. A mistle-thrush pecked at the hard ground; beyond them all, in a tree at the far side of the lawn, a magpie sat and watched the house.

It occurred to Andrew that it could do no harm to anyone if he just went out quickly and gave the birds last night's crusts and things, right there beside the house. Andrew knew that the birds couldn't pull worms out of the ground when it was all frozen hard; if people didn't feed them with other things, in this weather, the birds just starved and died. There was no reason that Andrew could see why they should go hungry and perhaps die just because it was Sunday. Or any reason why he shouldn't slip out there, just out and back quickly and not going anywhere except right beside the house, to take out a handful of crusts. His parents could hardly object to that. He wouldn't feed the guinea-pig, because it was farther from the house and took longer to do. He'd just take the crusts out and chuck them on the tin table and come straight back in and watch through this window again while the birds squabbled over the bits of food.

It would serve a good purpose and it would give him a way to pass the time until breakfast. There couldn't be any harm in that.

Andrew went into the kitchen and filled his pockets from the bowl that was kept near the bread-board; in the lobby he stepped into his rubber boots, and then he unlocked the back door very quietly and shut it again behind him just as gently. He stuck to his plan, went directly round the corner of the house and along the flagged path to the bird-table; the birds had all gone before he got to it, all except the robin which sat tight in the quince tree and watched him with a kind of impertinence while he emptied his pockets and spread the crusts and crumbs evenly over the surface of the table. Then he turned around, frowned at the robin, and went back the way he'd come; but at the corner he stopped and looked back, to see if the birds had begun to reassemble yet. The robin had started on the bread, all right. Andrew waited, just for a moment, to see which bird would be the first to join it. If it was a small bird, a sparrow especially, the robin would make a lunge at it, to scare it away; the sparrow could retreat temporarily, but by that time a lot of other birds would be joining in, and the robin would give up trying to hog it all for himself. Andrew just waited for a moment, to see that routine played out before he went back into the house.

No bird of any kind had joined the robin yet. Andrew glanced round the garden. It was completely empty, of course. The lawn was all frosted and there were no marks of any sort on its white surface. Beyond it, there was the gate to the paddock. If he went to that gate across the lawn, he'd leave his footprints for anyone to see the minute they looked out of the bathroom window. But if he went along the bricked path above the vegetable beds, and then turned down close against the hedge, he'd be able to get to the gate without leaving any tracks at all.

It would only be for a minute or two; and he knew that he wouldn't be allowed out here again, not once his parents were up. It might be days or even weeks before they'd let him out. He could just spend half a minute at that gate, thinking about his pony, and then go straight back into the house and up to his room. Then there wouldn't be so long, after that, to wait for breakfast, and it wouldn't be so dull, being shut in all day, because he'd have been out and he'd have this to think about.

He'd forgotten about the birds now. He went along the path to its end, past the side of the garage and right to the hedge that ran down between the garden and the paddock. Then he turned down and walked over the hard turf to the paddock gate. He stepped up on to its lowest bar and held on to the top one, and looked pleasurably around the paddock to see where his pony would be on a cold morning like this one.

Andrew glanced down to his left, at the stable, and looked away again: then he looked back quickly, open-mouthed with surprise. That stable door was shut! But it was always kept open. Someone had shut it; even from here Andrew could see that it was bolted. He wondered who on earth could have done that; nobody had any right to. That door was left open on purpose, to get the garage smell out of the stable, before the pony came.

There was nothing he could do except go down there right away and open the door himself. He couldn't just tell someone it was shut, because that would be to admit that he'd been down here at the gate; you couldn't see the stable door from any window in the house, or from any part of the garden. And he wouldn't get another chance to be out here. Andrew knew he had to go down to the stable now and open its door, before he went back into the house. He'd never intended to stay out this long, or to go so far from the house, and it frightened him that he had to, because he knew his father would be absolutely furious if he knew what he was doing; but, of course, his father *wouldn't* know. Even if he or his mother looked out of the bathroom window while he was doing it, they wouldn't see him on the other side of the hedge.

And he just had to. That was all there was to it.

He climbed quickly over the gate and hurried down the track towards the stable. The cinder surface was frozen hard and it didn't crunch as he walked on it. He got to the stable and at once set to work on the bolt; it was stiff, and as cold as ice, he had to bang at it and joggle it; it took all his strength and quite a little time before he could pull it back to free the door. Then the door was stiff, too, and as he dragged it open the hinges groaned loudly, frighteningly; but he told himself that the sound wouldn't carry to the house. Besides, his parents would still be fast asleep. Sometimes even the alarm clock, right beside their heads, didn't wake them—let alone a rusty hinge all this way off and outside the house.

He'd got the door right open. It was so stiffly held, with the hard, rough grass pushing up under it, and the hinges stiff as well, that he didn't bother about latching it back. He turned his back on the open door and went quickly up the track towards the gate. He was at the gate, actually on it and in the act of climbing over, when it struck him that he really should have latched that stable door. He'd been in too much of a hurry to have it done and get back to the house; now he wondered if he shouldn't go back—well, run back—and do the job properly. He paused, half across the gate, and looked back over his shoulder at the stable with its open door.

Just at that very moment a sound caught his ears: only a small one, but in the total silence of this early morning it was clear and definite, the sound of cracking branches. It seemed to have come from farther down the hedge above the stream; Andrew was on the gate with his head twisted to look over his right shoulder, so that he couldn't see, as he was, in the direction of the sound, which had come again, was in fact continuous. He let go of the gate and dropped to the ground, whirling to face that lower hedge.

The lion was coming up out of the stream, forcing its way through the straggly, leafless hedgerow. Its great head pushed through like a battering-ram: then the enormously deep chest, huge paws reaching forward as the lion came over the edge of the stream's steep bank and clear through the hedge; it moved quite slowly but in each movement there was a terrifying power, a power quite stunning in its effect on the boy who stood absolutely still with his back flat against the gate as if he'd been nailed there. His eyes were wide and staring and his mouth was open although in fact no breath came in or went out.

The lion didn't even glance at him. Its face and beard were streaming water; it moved slowly along the hedgerow with its head low to the ground, its eyes no more than slits. There were leaves and sticks and bits of dead bracken in its mane and stuck to its sides. The tufted end of its tail curved sharply upwards, just clearing the ground behind it; its ribs showed clearly, and as it walked its belly swung slowly from side to side.

Instead of keeping to the hedgerow now it was slanting into the paddock. When it seemed to notice the blank wall of the stable—the side of it—across its path, it turned out even more, so that it was heading, eventually, towards the gate where Andrew stood. But near that corner of the stable, on the edge of the cinder track, the lion seemed to hesitate. It swung its head away to the right, and stopped, its slitted amber eyes fixed on that dark slab of open doorway. It moved forward again, towards the stable.

Andrew watched the lion disappear: the last thing he saw was the tufted end of its tail as it went into the stable and swung aside inside the door.

Andrew's heart and pulses were pounding so hard that he felt as if he'd burst; his eyes were swimming and although he hadn't moved an inch he was shaking like a puppet on a jerky string.

He had to shut that door.

The lion had deliberately sought shelter in Andrew's pony's stable, and the door would have to be shut. If they caught it in there, they'd shoot it. His father had said so. It was incredible, but he'd said it.

If the door was shut, they wouldn't look inside. The lion could rest itself in there just as long as it wanted to; it would be safe, once the door was shut. When it wanted to leave, to move on to wherever it wanted to go, or to go back to wherever it had come from, it could get out easily enough (and for that matter back in again, if it wanted to) where the big wooden shutter was still latched open in the stable's lower side. That opening was in the very corner of the paddock, shielded and hidden; it was close to the stream, too, where the lion could drink when it was thirsty.

But the door had to be shut. It had been shut before, by someone, and now it must be shut again. Andrew thought suddenly of his parents; at any moment they'd be waking up, looking for him. He had to do it now, quickly, and get back into the house. To be caught here now would not only make trouble for him: it would lead to the discovery of the lion.

He ran, keeping on the narrow strip of turf between the hedge and the cinder track. Just as he got to the stable he heard a loud, heavy thump and a rasping, blowy sound as if the lion had been holding its breath and let all of it go at once. Then, as he slammed the door, finding a new strength in his own arms that surprised him, he heard a soft, deep growl, like a giant snoring in his sleep.

He jerked the bolt across, and ran.

V

O N SUNDAYS, just to remind themselves that they had one, the
Fowlers had breakfast in their dining-room. Andrew and
his father had eggs and bacon, and Susan ate toast and read
one of the papers, the one John Fowler called a rag and never
looked at.

Andrew was still shaking inside, and he wasn't at all hungry;
but he forced himself to eat everything his mother had given him,
because the last thing he wanted now was a fuss about temperatures and doctors and being off-colour. Well, he *was* off-colour.
He'd seen himself in the mirror in his bedroom, when he was
back up there and waiting for his parents to wake up; he'd been in
no hurry for that, not after what had happened and having such a
lot to think about; when Susan Fowler had eventually come
along to his room, in her dressing-gown, she'd been alarmed at
her son's pale face—just as she had been the day before.

"It's being shut up indoors," he'd told her. "If I could go
out in the garden, just for a bit, even—"

She'd shaken her head. "No, Andrew. It's a nuisance, I know,
but it won't be for long. Just until they catch the lion . . . Well,
hurry up and finish dressing. Breakfast'll be ready in a minute."

She kissed him on his forehead. When he'd got back to his
room he'd taken off some of his clothes and lain on the bed to
wait until they were up. That's how he'd been, staring at the
ceiling and quite lost in thought, when she'd come along to find
him. Anyway, she'd accepted his explanation for the lack of
colour in his cheeks, and there had been none of the usual rush
for a thermometer. His father had ruffled his hair and said, "If
we hear they've got that animal, we'll all go for a good long walk
across the fields. Eh?" Andrew had nodded, the slightest nod he

could give without seeming rude; it felt like telling a kind of lie, because he knew perfectly well that nobody was going to catch the lion. Now, at breakfast, he realised that for as long as the lion wasn't caught or killed, he'd be confined to the house. For a split second he imagined himself as a Judas, gaining his own liberty by betraying the lion to its executioners. He shivered.

"Sugar please, Andrew."

He passed it to his father, who'd just poured himself another half-gallon of coffee. He had a special cup not unlike a chamber pot. John Fowler was spooning sugar into it when the door-bell rang.

"What on earth—?" Susan asked him. "Will you go, or shall I?"

"I will." John Fowler rose, looking grim as he faced the early call. Andrew, at the window, told them, "It's Constable Williams. He's all red in the face."

"Oh!" Susan looked up at her husband as he passed her on his way to the door. "Come to tell us they've caught the lion, I expect. He said he'd be round to tell us." She said to Andrew, "We'll be able to have that walk now, old Paleface." She glanced at his plate, and smiled at him. "Nothing pale about your appetite, anyway."

Andrew felt quite sick. He strained his ears to hear what the policeman was telling his father, out in the hall. His voice was high and excited and it was going on and on. When he paused for breath Andrew heard his father ask a question, and the policeman's voice started up again at once.

"Toast and marmalade, Andrew?"

Andrew just looked at her. Her words flew over his head as he still tried to pick up even a word of the policeman's excited monologue.

"Andrew!"

He blinked at her. "Yes?"

"I asked if you wanted toast and marm—"

"No, thank you."

His father's voice now, briefly. The door opening and shutting: his father's footsteps, coming back this way.

John Fowler put his hand on his wife's shoulder as he passed her chair. He sat down in his own and Andrew and Susan watched him, waiting to hear what it was all about. For a few moments all he did was to stir his coffee.

"I did sugar this, didn't I?"

Andrew nodded. Susan Fowler asked her husband sharply, "Have they shot it?"

"No. Not yet. But they will soon. There's hundreds of soldiers coming to search all round."

"Round here?"

He nodded. "You know old Mrs Hailey, who works for those rather peculiar people—"

"The Reginalds. They aren't really peculiar."

He shrugged. "Well, Mrs Hailey isn't working for them this morning. She's in hospital."

Susan gasped. "*Not the lion?*" Her husband nodded. Andrew heard a sob coming out of his own mouth, and put a hand up to stop it. He couldn't stop the tears which he felt welling up in his eyes. His mother jumped up and went to him and put her arms round him, her face against his. "Darling, there's nothing to be frightened of. Don't cry."

"I'm *not* crying." He gasped the words out. "It's not true, they're lying—"

John Fowler said quickly, "The lion didn't touch her. It killed that dog of hers. She got away, somehow. She's suffering from shock, that's about all."

Andrew had suddenly quietened, and he seemed to be in control of himself. His mother let go of him, and straightened up. Standing behind his chair still, she asked her husband, "Where did it happen, and when?"

"Early this morning. Up on the top there, the footpath. You know. She comes over that way at God knows what hour, every morning, when it's still dark. On Sundays she's even earlier than other days, to finish her work before morning service. Don't you remember the Reginalds telling us about her?"

Susan nodded.

"As far as the police can gather from what she's been able to tell them so far, the lion just rushed up and bit the dog's head off. Mrs Hailey sprinted clear across two fields and through three thick thorn hedges. She was all torn and scratched, and screaming fit to bust. A newspaper roundsman found her—he was driving his van along the lane, went round one of those bends pretty fast, and there she was, reeling about in the middle of the road. He only just managed to brake short of her." Suddenly he began to laugh. Susan looked shocked, and he explained, "Be a bit hard on the old faggot to get bowled over by a van, after all that!"

Andrew laughed too. Susan frowned at them both. She asked John, "What else did Williams say?"

"Just that the army are coming. They've had troops waiting around for someone to get eaten so they'd know where to start the hunt."

"Those ones we saw yesterday, I suppose—"

"I suppose so. And all over the area. Now they're all being whistled up, tally-ho and follow the blood-stains—"

"John!"

Andrew said quietly, "I bet that dog attacked the lion first." Susan told him, "If you've drunk all your milk, you can get down." When they were alone she said to John, "Why on earth is he so much on the lion's side? He wasn't upset for poor Mrs Hailey, only that he thought you were saying it had gone for her. He said 'They're lying'—did you hear that?"

Her husband nodded.

"And now suggesting it was the dog's fault!"

John Fowler shrugged. "I suppose the lion's an impressive thing to him. King of the beasts, and all that. And it's alone, being hunted. He's imaginative, and it's got his sympathy." He chuckled. "It might have mine, if it didn't have four-inch teeth."

*   *   *

Cradling their FN .300 rifles before them (five rounds in each magazine, fifty in each soldier's bandolier) the men of B Company of the East Loamshires came in a long wavering line across the fields from the new building area near the Tunbridge Wells road at Langton. They were moving north, towards Farnham, to start with, more than a hundred men in line abreast, their breath rising like gunsmoke in the frozen air as they advanced steadily across fields, climbing fences, pushing through hedges. Their subalterns and NCOs, carrying Stens, strove more anxiously to keep the line straight than to spot the lion. Company HQ, Major Willesley with them, had taken up a position in their transport in the lane near Farnham; sentries had been posted along the verges of the lane to stop the lion if it attempted to break out downhill on the flank of the advancing riflemen. Platoon HQ's were in the line, their signalmen in touch by radio with the Company Commander down below and on their left. It was considered unlikely that the lion would get away to the right, because on that side the land was all built up and bare of natural growth; the lion, surely wanting open country, must retreat before them or break left. And it was there, all right; they all knew about Mrs Hailey.

In the centre of the line, No. 2 Section under Corporal Lanning made the first find. It was one of Mrs Hailey's shoes, lodged in a hedgerow. Higgins found it: Frith appreciated its importance.

"'Ere, Corp!" He held it up. "Must 'a come off that poor old bag, eh?" The other shoe was in the field, not a dozen yards away. Their positions indicated clearly Mrs Hailey's line of precipitate retreat, which coincided with No. 2 Section's line of advance. The signalman reported the finds to Company HQ, who acknowledged without enthusiasm. The line had moved on, and the Section had to break into an uphill trot to take the belly out of it.

When they slowed again, Frith told Higgins, "'Ere, Garbage. You spots it close up, and no time to shoot, you know what you do?"

Higgins glanced at him. "Run?"

Frith made a sound of disgust. He said in his officer's voice, sternly, "Run, my man? A soldier o' the Loamshires does not run—'cept after a bird, that is. No, mate: you looks it in the eye, fearless like."

He stumbled, and swore. Lanning shouted, "Watch it there!" Higgins muttered, "*Spit* in its eye, more likely."

At the top of the field, in the edge of some brush, Lanning found the fore-quarters of the dog, its front paws and shoulders and the remains of the crushed head, in a shallow pool of blood. Close by, they found a woman's shopping bag, and that was blood-stained too. Again they reported the find to Company HQ.

But there was no blood trail, which Lanning searched for; the lion must have had its snack on the spot, and moved on. There were no tracks either; even a soldier's boot left no imprint in the rock-hard ground, and the frost was uneven, dappled and patchy on the tufted fields.

The line of soldiers moved on, through woodland, over plough and grassland, skirting ice-topped pools. Its left was always in contact with the hedgerow of the lane. As the line advanced, the sentries in the lane were moved up too; and Company HQ in its APV moved up too, rumbling towards Rusthall along the winding, icy lane. The front was narrowing and the line of Loamshires contracted as it moved forward and swung east.

*   *   *

From the window of the spare bedroom, Andrew watched the soldiers. He saw the left wing of the line of riflemen as they crossed the field opposite, on the other side of the lane, and he saw the sentries in the lane and the HQ vehicle, which at one time was stopped almost right outside the house. There were sentries out there too, for a bit; they stood with their backs to the house, watching the high slope of field as the other soldiers crossed it slowly from right to left. Then the whole lot moved on, out of sight; later a whole convoy of empty truck things — they were APVs, and Andrew's mother told him they were armoured cars — growled past, heading in the same direction.

Normally Andrew would have been thrilled to see it all; he would have waved to the soldiers, storing up everything in his mind to pass on to his school friends, on Monday. But as it was, he stood well back from the window so that none of them would see him watching.

He was on the other side. Not by choice. He just was.

Then it was time to get tidied up for church. John Fowler, when he was ready, took the shotgun with him to the garage, kept it under his arm while he unlocked the doors and opened the double gates to the lane; then he got in the car and backed it out and parked it in the lane opposite the front door, where there'd be the shortest possible distance for Susan and the boy to walk. He walked with them, carrying the gun, from the front door to the car; then he took the cartridges out of the gun and passed it in to Andrew, in the back, before he got in himself. Andrew didn't say a word; he put the gun down on the floor, and looked at it all the way to church.

Nobody was standing round outside, as they usually did, chatting about the weather and their gardens until it was time to go in for the service. And inside, there were fewer people than usual. Andrew sat between his father and mother, found the place in the Prayer Book and sat still, staring at his knees. Nobody had to tell him not to fidget. Even when the service started, he kept his eyes down; he didn't want to look at anyone. There were so few people that hardly anyone sang the hymns loudly enough for their voices to be heard; only the organ and the Vicar's croak were audible.

The text of the sermon was from Judges xiv, 14:

> *Out of the eaten came forth meat,*
> *And out of the strong came forth sweetness.*

The congregation stiffened, and stared in obvious consternation at the Vicar. He spoke about the War, and about comradeship in the face of adversity: referred to the Home Guard and the Navy and the Battle of Britain and the bombing of London, and went on to assert that a danger to the community drew people of all sorts and conditions together and brought out the best in all of them. Later he read a special prayer for the quick recovery of their beloved sister Henrietta Hailey. Andrew said his own prayer, his lips moving silently under folded hands during the Blessing: *God, please don't let them shoot the lion.*

Then it was over. The Vicar stood in the porch, not outside

as he usually did when it wasn't raining. Nobody stopped long to talk; they nodded at him, smiling nervously, and hurried out, glancing quickly round the churchyard as they passed between the ancient gravestones to the gate.

On the way home John Fowler said cheerfully, "Not much of a turn-out, was it?"

Susan just nodded. John said, "You'd think they were expecting it to be hiding in the font." He turned the car gently into the lane. Over his shoulder he told Andrew, "I didn't hear you doing much singing, old chap."

His mother answered quickly for him. "I thought Andrew was specially good today." She added, "I didn't hear anyone, except the poor old Vicar. I certainly didn't hear you, John."

"I only give tongue when there's so much row nobody could possibly hear me. You know that."

Susan Fowler laughed. "That's on Remembrance Sunday. The only day of the year Grandfather Kenney would ever come with us."

Andrew remembered that. The old man always wore one of the big poppies, the kind meant to go on the fronts of cars; and he'd spend the rest of the day talking about that first war and the trenches and naming his friends who'd died in or between them. Andrew could still hear quite plainly the old man's voice growling, "They died for you, boy. Never forget that. Never forget it."

He never would forget it. He wouldn't have, even if Grandfather Kenney hadn't told him not to. He only hoped that one day he'd know why.

Jesus had died for him too. If Andrew had been there at the times these things had happened, and had had any influence, he'd have asked them not to. It had simply happened, and he was told about it and none of it made sense.

Surprisingly few things did.

At lunch, his father asked him suddenly if he'd like them to have a mink farm, here where they lived. Andrew liked the idea of having any kind of farm, so he said yes, he would, he'd love it. His mother looked quite sharply at his father.

"Andrew doesn't even know what a mink is—he's certainly never seen one. How can he say he'd like them?"

His father smiled at him, and said, "Like ferrets, only bigger and different colours—sable, pearl—all kinds. We'd have a few to start with, and soon hundreds, in cages, and you could help me look after them."

"I'd like that. Do they have to stay in their cages all the time?"

Susan Fowler said, looking not at him but at his father, "They'd be in the paddock, Andrew. All over it. And their food would be kept in the stable."

At the mention of the stable, Andrew felt himself blushing scarlet. His face burned with it and in his embarrassment he dropped his fork; it clattered loudly on the plate in front of him.

Nobody told him he was clumsy, or to be more careful. He grabbed the fork up quickly, not looking at either of his parents. John Fowler murmured, "It's only an idea, Andrew. I haven't decided on it yet."

*   *   *

From time to time during the afternoon Andrew went upstairs to look out of the windows on all sides of the house, one after another, for any sign of the soldiers. But when they did come back, not much short of tea-time, they came not over the fields but along the lane, in their transports.

The growing rumble of engines brought Andrew and his mother to the windows of the drawing-room, which was on that side of the house. John Fowler was in his study, working. Either he didn't hear or he was too busy to care about it.

They could see one of the APVs parked close to the bend of the lane where it led round to Rusthall. Another had stopped right opposite their own garage gates, and a third was just visible through the leafless thorn hedge which divided the upper lawn from the lane's wide, grass verge. By the time Andrew and Susan Fowler got to the windows of the drawing-room, soldiers were jumping down and milling about close to their trucks; and before they'd had time to take in what was happening or even to call John Fowler to come and look, another of those strange-looking vehicles shot up quite fast and swerved in to stop right in front of the house.

One of the officers was quite old, like Andrew's father. He said something to the other one, and then turned and stared at the house. He saw Susan Fowler at once, and he saluted, smiling broadly.

The officer jumped down into the lane and came straight through the gate towards the front door. Susan Fowler didn't wait for the bell to ring; she glanced quickly round the room, picked up a cushion and dropped it, patted another cushion, then put up her arms and patted at her hair too as she went out into the hall to open the front door. Just as the bell rang she was passing through the door to the hall; Andrew called to her, "Shall I get Daddy?"

His mother didn't hear him, probably because he'd spoken while the bell was ringing. Andrew went to tell his father what was happening.

When Susan Fowler opened the door, Major Willesley saluted her again, and smiled. She asked him, "Won't you come in?"

"Thanks awfully, but I really mustn't."

"Well—"

"What a pretty house you have. I saw it earlier, but I hadn't realised—frightfully pretty . . . I—is your husband in, Mrs— er—?"

"Fowler. Yes." She called into the house, "John, can you come?"

The soldier said, "We *are* in a bit of a hurry. The light, you know."

"The light?" She had no idea what he was talking about. "You haven't found the lion yet?"

"'Fraid not. The brute's not on *that* side"—Willesley waved a hand behind him—"and he's not that way either." He jerked his head towards the north. "So now I want to cover as much of the ground on your side as I can before it gets dark. After that it'll be pretty hopeless, you know."

Susan felt a hand on her shoulder, and at the same moment the soldier's smile became more formal, more courteous and less gallant. His tone was different too, flatter, as he put out his hand and asked unnecessarily, "Mr Fowler?"

"Yes." Susan stood aside, and the two men looked at each other. John Fowler asked, "Aren't you coming in?" Willesley shook his head. "I was just telling your wife, we've got to push on with it. Fact is, I want some of my chaps to pass through your garden—then up that hill behind you, you see, and at the top we'll swing left and back towards Langton Green. I've got men on the Speldhurst road in case the animal charges out that way."

John Fowler nodded, and stepped out of the door. Susan saw that he had his shotgun under his arm. He told her, "I won't be long. Stay inside."

The soldier flashed her a quick smile, and raised his hand. "Good-bye, Mrs Fowler. Thank you so much. And don't worry —we'll find the beast!"

John Fowler led Major Willesley along the front of the house and into the open space between it and the timber garage, above the vegetable beds. He saw groups of soldiers waiting all along the lane, one lot right by the garage gates. Willesley asked him, "Are any of these surrounding fields yours?"

"Only that small paddock. Look—all along the bottom there, there's a stream, with steep banks. I suppose you'll want your men to search it, but they'll cross more easily at that far end of the paddock, and at the other end, from that boggy field. There are plank bridges, you see, in both places."

"Ah." They were approaching the paddock gate. The Major said, "I'll start them off, then, if you don't mind." He turned to face the road, and shouted, pointing out the bridges. The younger officer waved acknowledgement: whistles blew, soldiers flooded into the garden, spread out to left and right. John Fowler and Major Willesley pushed the paddock gate open, and went through. Soldiers filed through behind them and began searching along the inside of the upper hedge. In the lane the APV's were turning, edging forward and back to face the other way.

"This—er—stable?"

"Yes. Was a garage. As a matter of fact, I'm thinking of

starting a mink farm in this field, and using that for their food and stuff." He wondered why he'd mentioned it. Probably because it was on his mind.

Willesley might have been wondering the same thing. He glanced at him, and coughed. "Really. Minks, eh? Capital." He coughed again. "But"—he pointed at the stable—"I mean, we'd better take a shufti inside, eh? No stones unturned, and all that."

John Fowler stopped at the stable and leant with his shoulder against the door. He shook his head.

"I've saved you that trouble. This door's been shut and bolted since I checked the place myself."

The soldiers came down across the paddock and the garden to the next line of cover, which was the hedge above the stream. John Fowler and Major Willesley stood together by the corner of the stable, watching them. The Major said, "If we don't flush it on this sweep—by the time we get back to the main road, that is—I'm back to square one. I had to assume that the beast was in this area, lying-up after it liquidated that dog. If it took off, though, nipped over the lane somewhere—and damn it, it was still dark then, you know—and pushed off westward—well, it could be miles away by now."

He looked more angry than thoughtful. John Fowler nodded. "I suppose it could." He watched one of the soldiers struggling to disentangle his Combat Dress from the strands of barbed wire that lined the hedge. "But the more it moves about, the more chance there is of someone spotting it. You'll get another report of it pretty soon, I dare say."

"Wrong sort of report—that's what I'm scared of." Willesley frowned at him. "Got children here?"

"I've a son."

"Well, keep a tight rein on him. This lion's dangerous. An old one—can't chase things much. When they get old, in the wild, people are the easiest game for them."

"Sheep don't take much catching, do they? And they've got lambs now."

"There's that. Yes. Still, better be safe than sorry." Willesley said briskly, "Well, I must be getting along. Thanks for letting us cross your land. And don't worry—we're as anxious to get this over as you are. Ought to be in Nicosia by now, damn it. Well, good-bye, Mr—er—"

"Fowler."

"Yes, of course. Were you in the army, Mr Fowler?"

"Air Force. But I was still in training when the war ended."

"Oh, bad luck. Damn bad luck." Willesley laughed. "Better luck next time, eh?"

*   *   *

Upstairs, at the bathroom window, Andrew watched the Major leave his father and stride up over the cinders through the paddock gate. The soldiers had finished poking about on the other side of the stream; they were moving up the hillside now, a line of them that stretched right across three fields.

For a minute or two, it had looked as if the Major and his father were going into the stable. Andrew had stood frozen with anxiety: first for the discovery of the lion, then for what it might do to his father if he blundered in and frightened it. He'd been on the point of throwing the window open and shouting a warning to them, when incredibly he'd seen his father lean against the stable door and turn and talk to the Major as if he was stopping him from going in.

Andrew had waited, watching every move that either of them made, terrified that at any moment one of them would make up his mind to pull back the bolt and drag the door open.

But they hadn't. Andrew knew that he'd never understand why. He looked up at the field again; the soldiers were half-way up it now, the whole long line of them crossing the path the lion had taken when he'd first seen it in the moonlight and it had stopped and stared at him as if it had known that he'd be there. It felt like something that had happened a month ago, instead of only a couple of days.

VI

Monday mornings were always more rushed than the other four; getting out of bed at six-thirty wasn't easy after the enjoyed pleasure of Saturday and Sunday, and when he did get out, five or ten minutes later than he should have, John Fowler shaved and dressed faster than was really possible—not only to make up the lost time, but also because he had by this stage realised that it was Monday, with its traffic into London worse than on any other day. It was a day to start early, rather than late.

And this morning he was worried, doubtful of every hasty move even as he made it. He felt he ought to be staying at home, to keep an eye on Susan and Andrew as long as the lion was loose, to cope with any emergency that might develop. He had the portable radio on, talking rubbish at him while he shaved and dressed, but there was no mention of the lion-at-large. If it had been shot, there would surely have been an announcement.

"The military must have drawn a blank."

Susan told him not to worry. "They searched all round here, and if it had been anywhere near they'd have found it. I expect it was miles away before they even started."

He grunted, and put down his razor. He was thinking that the animal could have been lying doggo in some ditch they hadn't looked in. As that soldier had said, 'better safe than sorry'. Until it was shot, the lion was a danger. And a man's responsibility was to protect his family from danger. Living in England, there wasn't any—except perhaps to their morals. (Thank God Andrew was a boy!) Life was sheltered, civilised: they didn't even have typhoons or earthquakes. Yet now there *was* a danger, and he felt it, the threat to his wife and child. But in this sheltered life the wolf-pack was commercial and financial; he had the responsibilities of the breadwinner. Today he had a lunch date with the chief executive of a huge overseas concern; there was a chance he could pull off something really big. If he missed the lunch, there'd certainly be no deal, there might even be a loss of business that existed already; and he could imagine how his Managing Director would react if he told him that he'd had to stay at home because a lion had got out of a circus.

At breakfast, to save time, he had only one egg. Then he got Susan's car out of the garage and brought it up into the lane, opposite the front door. He fed the guinea-pig too. Back in the house, he told Susan, "Keep the car there in the lane, darling. Don't put it away: I'll do that when I get home. Just go straight between the car and the front door, and nowhere else—"

She'd started to laugh. He told her, "And don't hang about outside. If there's anything at all, ring me at once, and I'll come back."

She said, smiling, "Yes, Daddy." Andrew didn't look up from his egg. He'd hardly spoken, this morning. He was all ready for school, his hair shiny from the brush.

"Well." John Fowler squeezed his son's shoulder as he passed behind his chair. He kissed Susan. "You may think it's a joke, but just do as I say, will you?"

She promised him, "We'll be careful. Don't worry." She called after him, "Good luck with your lunch!"

*   *   *

When Susan Fowler had done the washing-up and made the beds with Andrew's help, it was time to get him to school. They put their coats on and went out of the front door and straight to the car, as John Fowler had told them to, walking quickly. Susan had laughed at her husband's warnings: but now that he'd gone she was lonely without him and did exactly as he'd said. She pushed Andrew into the car on the near side and slid in after him as he squirmed over to the other seat, and she shut the door as soon as she was in.

At the school she got out and took him right to the door. All the other mothers were doing the same thing, shoo-ing their children in, then hurrying back to their cars. Some, who operated in syndicates, brought coveys of three or four children besides their own. All the mothers smiled at each other with the same brittle intensity; even mothers who didn't know or like each other. *Out of the strong,* Susan remembered wryly, *came forth sweetness.* In the original, it had been honey; this was saccharin. The children were far more honest, they simply glared at each other and shoved their way inside.

When Andrew went into the cloakroom to hang up his coat and change his shoes, and saw his friend Peter Wale there, standing on one leg and doing the same thing, he was so glad to see him that he hit him as hard as he could between the shoulder-blades and shouted "Got you!" Peter Wale shot forward, right into the line of hanging coats and shoe-bags; he struggled to his feet and out of a heap of fallen coats with a look of fury on his small, pugnacious face; when he saw who it was that had hit him he let out a cowboy whoop and struck Andrew in the chest with both fists at once. Andrew reacted in an entirely natural way: he punched his friend in the stomach with his left fist, and slapped him hard across the head with his open right hand.

Neither of them liked anyone else very much, but they were good friends and fought whenever they could. Unfortunately there wasn't time, now, to get on with it. Peter just pushed Andrew away, using all his strength, so that Andrew staggered back, knocking Jeremy Clark hard against the wall and thus, luckily, cushioning his own impact on it so that he didn't bang his head, which he certainly would have done if Jeremy hadn't been there.

Jeremy Clark, who was bigger than either Andrew or Peter, let out a squawk and began to shout complaints in a high, ringing tone, so Peter Wale pushed him against the wall again, and told him crossly that it had been his own fault for getting in the way. The other children were sensibly skirting round them, giving them the widest berth that space permitted, as they hurried into the classrooms. The teachers were already in there, waiting.

Peter Wale turned his back on Jeremy Clark, and said to Andrew, "Come on. Or she'll be yelling at us."

Andrew nodded. He said, "All right. But I've got something to tell you about."

"What?"

"There isn't time now. It's a long thing."

"Tell me in break, then." Peter looked interested. "Or whisper it when she isn't looking."

Andrew shook his head. "I'll tell you in break."

"All right."

They were the last to take their places in class, after Prayers, and the teacher commented on it, ending with the words 'as usual'. Andrew and Peter glanced at each other and smiled self-consciously, as if they'd just been congratulated or paid a compliment.

In the break, they were surprised to be allowed outside. They weren't allowed far from the building, though, or off on their own, or anywhere near the bluebell wood. It hadn't got bluebells in it yet, anyway. Peter Wale beckoned Andrew after him, winked, and walked importantly to the farthest corner of the yard.

When Andrew came up to him, Peter just stared into his face and waited. Andrew stared back, ready to put his guard up.

"Well?"

Andrew frowned. "What d'you mean, *well*?"

"What's this thing you're going to tell me?"

"Oh, that." Andrew looked away. "Yes, well—well, I'm not."

"What d'you mean, you're not? Not what?"

"Not going to tell you. It isn't anything much, anyway."

"Then why did you start telling me about it?"

"I didn't. I was just thinking that I *might* tell you. And I'm not going to, after all."

Peter Wale reached out and tapped Andrew on his shoulder. He said, conversationally, "If you don't tell me, I'll break your neck."

"Go on and try, then!" Andrew grinned. He stepped closer

to his friend, raising his fists. "Go on, try!" One of the teachers called out shrilly, "Andrew! Andrew Fowler!"

He turned and looked at her. "Yes, Miss Wilmott?"

"None of that brawling, now. Nor you, Peter. Behave yourselves, both of you!"

After a pause, during which they gazed at Miss Wilmott and then at each other as if they hadn't any idea at all what she'd been talking about, Peter Wale muttered, "Well, you'd better tell me anyway, if you know what's good for you. What's it about?"

Andrew said, "I might tell you. Tomorrow, or on Wednesday. It depends."

He was longing to talk about the lion, and Peter Wale was the only person he could possibly confide in. But if he told him, Peter might just conceivably tell someone else. Then the news might get around, and the soldiers would come back, and this time they'd know where to look.

The trouble was, Andrew had no way of knowing if the lion had left the stable and moved on somewhere else. He couldn't go down there to see: he wasn't allowed out of the house, and even if his parents relaxed that discipline he wouldn't want to draw attention to the stable by going down to it.

Sooner or later he'd have to tell Peter Wale the whole story. Not only for the sake of getting it off his chest, having someone else in the secret with him; together they'd be able to talk the thing over and work out a plan of action.

But he wasn't ready to tell him yet. He wouldn't know where to start, because it was all so confused in his own mind. Grandfather Kenney was in it, somewhere; then there was the way the lion had stopped on the hillside and looked at him, and the way it had walked into the stable when he'd opened the door; and finally there was his father stopping the soldiers from going into the stable.

It was all tied up in his mind like a string full of knots. The more he thought about it, the more tangled it got.

Andrew took a firm grip on Peter Wale's wrist with his own two hands, and began to twist that arm until Peter was all bent over and trying to lash out at Andrew with his feet to make him stop. Andrew told him, panting with the effort and jumping about to dodge the kicks, "I'll tell you tomorrow. It's about this lion they're looking for. I've got it hidden in our stable."

VII

WHEN JOHN FOWLER got home that evening he found Andrew in pyjamas and dressing-gown eating a supper of bananas and cream in front of the television set. Susan, who was sitting beside him on the sofa with sewing in her lap, looked searchingly into her husband's face.

"How did it go?"

He'd known the question was coming, but it was impossible to answer. All the way down from London, hardly noticing the road or the traffic, he'd reviewed his lunch and talk with the buyer from abroad, trying to work out for himself whether it had gone well or badly. At moments, it looked good; then he'd think of something he hadn't said, or something the other man *had* said, and he'd read a meaning into that and begin to think he'd botched it.

Susan's expression was eager as she looked up at him. He shrugged. "So so. Oh, pretty well, I think." He tousled Andrew's hair. "How's the boy?"

She frowned. Her husband knew darned well what she wanted to know, and he was holding out on her. He asked her, "Any news of the lion?"

"The what?" She gazed at him as dully as he had at her a moment ago.

He said slowly, "There is a lion, my sweet, a wild and carnivorous beast, roaming the Kentish pastures. Did no one tell you about this?"

"Oh, that. Well, Constable Williams came round this afternoon. He didn't have much to say."

"What did he come for, then?"

"Oh, I don't know. Just seeing we're all right, I suppose.

He did mention, in passing as it were, that the lion had been seen at Ashurst."

"Ah!" John Fowler sat down and took hold of one of his wife's hands. She withdrew it at once.

"Touching—but I'm trying to sew. A woman's work, and all that."

He sat back and studied her expression. "Have I done something I shouldn't?"

"How would *I* know? Andrew, as soon as this programme's over you're going to bed." Andrew nodded, his mouth full of banana, his eyes on the screen. Susan told her husband, "Constable Williams said the lion had been seen at Ashurst by some woman who's a Block Warden, whatever that is, for the Conservative Party. So she ought to be reliable, he said, but there've been some lambs killed at Poundsbridge and that looks like lion's work too."

"How much does Constable Williams know about lion's work?"

"He said that one of the lambs was bitten clean in half. He said it could have been dogs, but nobody ever saw a dog do *that* before. He seemed a bit confused, really."

John Fowler thought for a moment. Then he said, "Ashurst is about three miles west, and Poundsbridge is a mile north-west. So they're about two miles apart, roughly. I don't see why a lion couldn't bite a dozen lambs in half, if it wanted to, at Poundsbridge, then nip over to Ashurst and scare the daylights out of your Tory worker. . . . What did it do, chase her?"

"She just saw it, and it 'made off'. That's all Williams knew. D'you want any more to eat, Andrew?"

"No, thank you."

"Bed then."

Andrew nodded. He climbed down off the sofa and switched off the television. John Fowler offered, "I'll take you up on my back, if you like." He crouched down, waiting for the boy to leap up on his shoulders: it was a routine. But no weight landed as it usually did, with thin arms wrapping themselves round his neck. John Fowler looked round, and saw that his son was struggling out of the dressing-gown.

"What's this for?"

Andrew flung the dressing-gown across his father's back. He said, "Saddle. Ready?" On the way up, he said, "The lion wouldn't bite a lamb in half and leave it. Only if it was hungry, and then it would eat it too."

"How d'you know that?"

"It's obvious."

After the boy was in bed, the Fowlers came downstairs, and John poured drinks. He pulled a small table in front of the sofa, where Susan was already back at her sewing, and put the glasses on it before he flopped down beside her and began to fill a pipe. He told her, "I think it went off all right."

She didn't look up. "Hm?"

"My business lunch. No disaster, anyway."

"What did you have?"

"Have?"

"To eat."

"Oh, a chicken thing. Very good."

"It had garlic in it."

There was a pause then. John Fowler broke it, when he'd got the pipe going. He said, "You don't look like a wife at all. You look like someone's girl-friend. You're the most attractive thing I've seen all day."

Susan Fowler tucked the needle into whatever it was she was working on, put it all down on the arm of the sofa and looked up at him as she reached for her own drink.

"I feel like a wife." She sighed. "You really don't know yet?"

John shook his head. "He's got other people to see. The opposition. He'll be getting in touch later in the week. Has there been any sign of the military today?"

"No. Williams said they were all over at Ashurst, poor things."

"What's poor about them?"

"Well, plodding across a lot of dreary fields day after day — and after a lion that probably isn't there at all."

John Fowler drained his glass and put out his hand for hers

as well, to get fresh ones. He said, "Of course it's there. Somewhere. It can't have vanished into thin air. What d'you think
ate Mrs Hailey's dog—a rabbit?"

*   *   *

On Tuesday, Andrew got to school several minutes late; he'd
missed Prayers, and he rushed into the classroom just as Miss
Wilmott was starting the lesson. She stopped talking, and stared
at him in silence while he apologised and then hurried to the
back of the room and settled in his place. All the children twisted
round, too, and stared. Then, when Miss Wilmott began talking
again, all of them except Peter Wale stopped looking at him and
turned back to pay attention to what she was trying to teach
them.

Peter Wale went on staring at the side of Andrew's head. He
was sitting right beside him, as usual, and the close stare—which
Andrew could see out of the corner of his eye while he faced
Miss Wilmott and tried to take in what she was saying—was
extremely irritating. If he could have done it without Miss
Wilmott seeing, Andrew would have cracked his friend on the
nose, or something, to make him turn away. As it was, he simply
had to endure it, glowering and uneasy, until Miss Wilmott
noticed what was going on and told Peter Wale sharply to sit up
and not play the fool. Andrew looked round at him, then, and
nodded curtly, to let him know that he shared Miss Wilmott's
views on the way he'd been behaving.

Presently she had to turn her back on the class, in order to
write quite a long poem on the blackboard, so that later they
could copy it into their books. As soon as she'd turned away
from them, Peter hissed into Andrew's ear,

"How's the lion getting on?"

Andrew scowled at him and put his left hand over his ear, so
that if Peter Wale asked any more questions he wouldn't be able
to hear them. He hoped, in fact, that Peter would realise this
and not ask any. But it didn't work out like that, and knowing
Peter Wale as well as he did Andrew should have known it
wouldn't. What Peter did was to grab hold of Andrew's left

wrist in order to pull his hand off that ear, so that he could put his
question again.

Andrew fought him off, all right, but in doing so he somehow
flung himself sideways and knocked his head on the wall on his
right. His head hit the wall so hard that it made a loud thumping
sound, and Miss Wilmott whipped round and stared at him in
alarm, her chalky fingers poised in mid-air. Andrew just sat
bolt upright and stared back at her as if he was wondering what
it was she wanted; Peter Wale, on the other hand, kept looking
round him, up and down and from side to side, as if he was wondering where that thumping noise had come from and thought
he might catch it again, in the act.

Miss Wilmott knew perfectly well that it wouldn't do any
good to start questioning them. She'd tried that often enough,
without getting anywhere except making herself angry. She gave
Andrew a hard, suspicious glare, then turned back to the board to
finish chalking up the lines of verse.

Out of the corner of his eye Andrew could see that Peter Wale
was now busily drawing something on a loose page out of the
back of his exercise book; presently, with nonchalance and stealth,
Peter took the sheet of paper off his own desk and moved his arm
along out of sight so that the paper suddenly popped up again in
front of Andrew, right under his nose. He didn't touch it, just
stared at it, frowning, as if he had no idea where it had come
from or what it was supposed to represent.

It was a drawing of a lion. Just that, and a very large question-
mark beside it. Andrew shrugged his shoulders, and covered
the sheet of paper up with his own exercise book, and just then
Miss Wilmott finished writing on the blackboard and turned to
face them. She began to talk about the poem; Andrew listened
carefully to every word she spoke.

When the bell rang outside and the class rose, Andrew handed
the drawing back to its creator. He told him, "It's some kind
of dog all right, but I can't guess which."

By moving fast then, leaving Peter with his mouth open at
first in surprise and then shut tight in fury, and by hurrying up
to Miss Wilmott to ask her things about the poem until it was

time to start work again, Andrew managed to keep his friend at a distance.

Andrew wished fervently that he hadn't mentioned anything about the lion to Peter Wale. He hadn't meant to; it had just slipped out before he'd known it was coming, straight out of his wound-up mind via his flapping tongue. He'd been dying to talk to someone about it, and Peter Wale was just about the only one he could confide in; but he'd decided that he wouldn't, not anyway for several days, and now he had, and Peter's curiosity had of course been fired. It wasn't every day that someone you knew had a lion shut up where you could expect to go and look at it.

Andrew wished not only that he'd kept his mouth shut, but also that he hadn't opened it just as he had. That bit should have been worked up to gradually. There was so much more to it, such a depth of things he needed to understand properly himself before he could explain it all to someone else. It was all compounded of images, some that he'd seen with his eyes and some that he'd got in his head. Just to say "I've got the lion in my stable" wasn't saying anything at all. It was like saying "Grandfather Kenney won't be down to breakfast." That was true too, but it ignored many other things which were absolutely basic to any kind of understanding. And Grandfather Kenney was the only person to whom it would have been natural and easy to explain the whole of this.

But that was going round in circles. Grandfather Kenney was somehow a part of the story, and that was why he wasn't here to talk to. What was quite certain was that Peter Wale wasn't any kind of substitute for him, not in any sense. There was no question of thinking that Peter Wale's interest and curiosity could be as valuable as Grandfather Kenney's interest and wisdom would have been.

But, of course, he couldn't stall his friend for ever, and at lunch-time they met face to face. Andrew was feeling a bit guilty and furtive at having avoided Peter and his questions. Now, nose to nose with him, Peter Wale's eyes boring into his, he blushed and swallowed in embarrassment.

Ten minutes later, standing close together on the edge of the playing area where the other children were rushing around and screaming, the two boys were still deep in conversation. Andrew had blurted it all out, every single thing about it, and Peter Wale was absolutely fascinated.

"D'you think it's a kind of ghost, then?"

Andrew frowned at him. "No, of course not!" He'd known he wouldn't be able to explain it properly. How could he explain how the lion looked to him as it stalked like a king across the field in the moonlight, or how his heart had leapt and his mind froze into a solid chunk of exultation when it stopped and swung its head and stared at him? He snapped angrily at Peter Wale, "A ghost couldn't eat a dog up—and it wouldn't make a thump when it lay down."

"I suppose not. But if it's not a ghost, what—"

Andrew interrupted him. Jeremy Clark was edging close to them, with Hilda Patterson closing in on the other side. They were as thick as thieves, and Hilda had put it about that they were engaged to be married; more than that, they were persistent eavesdroppers, and they plainly had their ears cocked as they sidled up. Andrew muttered quickly, "I just don't know. I don't even know if it's still in there. I can't go down and look, either, so it's no good going on and on asking me questions about it." He raised his voice: "What do *you* want, Jeremy Clark?"

Jeremy, who was practically rubbing himself up against them by now, looked up in feigned surprise.

"Me? Oh—well, I found your drawing, and—"

"Drawing? What drawing?"

"It was on the floor so I picked it up. A drawing of a lion with a question by it. If you don't want it I'll colour it and pin it up at home in my room. It's super."

Andrew and Peter looked at each other. Andrew said, "I suppose he means that dog you drew. It did look a bit like a lion. You aren't very good at drawing, are you?"

Jeremy Clark sniggered. "This isn't a dog, it's a lion."

Peter nodded; there was a gratified look on his face. Andrew kicked him quite hard on the shin, and almost shouted, "It's a dog—*isn't it?*"

For a moment it hung in the balance; then Peter nodded crossly. "Oh, *that* one. Yes, that's a dog, all right. Even if it does look a bit like a lion."

*　　*　　*

John Fowler was late home that evening, too late to say good-night to Andrew, who was fast asleep when he crept in to see him. He didn't give Susan any details of what had kept him late, and she didn't ask about it. He seemed tense, and tired, and she put it down to the business of waiting for news of that export contract.

The television news programme brought both of them wide awake. It showed the East Loamshires on their lion hunt, search-ing the golf course and the Common at Holtye, where apparently the lion had been heard roaring that morning by a groundsman searching for lost balls. The soldiers had been at Ashurst the day before, the announcer said, doing the same thing after a local resident had actually seen the animal in a farmyard. A reporter interviewed her, a Mrs Weatherhead; when she tried to get in a plug for her Party, they cut her off, and switched over to interviews with farmers who'd had lambs killed at Chiddingstone Hoath, Eridge Green, Speldhurst, Groombridge and Fordcombe; each of the farmers swore it wasn't dogs' work. At this point in the programme they filled the screen with a blown-up map, with a cross on each of the places that had been mentioned; the crosses made a rough circle, and it struck John Fowler that they were sitting just about in its centre. He glanced at Susan, but she didn't say anything, and the programme switched back to the East Loamshires, ending with a close-up of Major Willesley, who told the viewing millions in a brisk, soldierly manner that a definite pattern was emerging and that he expected to finish the job within forty-eight hours.

John Fowler agreed with Andrew that a lion would hardly be slaughtering lambs just for the fun of it; whatever the farmers said, it seemed more likely to be dogs running wild, which was by no means uncommon at lambing-time. If you ruled out those farms, only Ashurst and Holtye remained as possibly valid reports: and that would mean that the search ought to be moving west, towards East Grinstead.

He was glad it wasn't his job to decide. It seemed extraordinary that a large and unusual thing like a lion could remain at large for so long with so many men out looking for it.

VIII

BY THURSDAY, John Fowler was really on edge, waiting for news of his export contract. He had it so much on his mind that he hardly thought about the lion at all; Susan had told him on Wednesday night that the soldiers had been back, beating all the hedgerows on the hillside during the morning and then streaming past the house, down the lane, in a long convoy of trucks that afternoon; he'd nodded, but that was all, it was a fact and she'd told him and he'd gone on thinking about the other thing. Sooner or later the lion would be caught; whether he'd catch that contract was far less certain and in the long run very much more important.

He thought now, I should have talked more about business and less about minks. When other salesmen have business lunches they probably talk shop all the time, even with their mouths full, and have a contract under the table ready for signature when their guests go ga-ga over the third large Cognac. I'm too soft to be a salesman; with a man like Jeffries you've got to put your foot in the door and beat him about the head until he comes to terms. A man of his stamp doesn't want to hear about mating minks.

He kept glancing at the telephone on his desk, willing it to ring. It did, several times; but each time it was some routine matter of no interest at all. He was beginning to think that Jeffries wouldn't telephone at all; he'd made up his mind days ago, probably; by the time he said good-bye after that dreary luncheon he'd already decided that he could do better somewhere else. Saying that he'd be in touch had been no more than a polite brush-off; there'd be no contract, and the present rate of ordering would gradually dwindle. And John Fowler would very likely get the sack.

But at twelve minutes past eleven, when his secretary had just put a cup of coffee on his desk, the telephone rang and he picked it up without any of the earlier hopes, and it was Jeffries.

"Mr Jeffries! How are you?"

The secretary looked startled: he'd positively yelled into the mouthpiece, and he'd half risen to his feet in excitement. He waved her off, and his right hand moved automatically to pick up a pencil and draw a note-pad closer.

"Well, that's fine, I'm glad. Very glad. . . . Yes, you're right, it really does look as if spring's arrived. Mr Jeffries, you've— you've seen all the people you planned to see, now?"

Jeffries said well no, he hadn't. He had to see an outfit up in Glasgow, and he was flying up there today, leaving his hotel in just a few minutes, blast it. He'd only rung to let John Fowler know that he'd be out of town for a couple of days. He'd be back late on Saturday, maybe not until Sunday. He'd be in touch then, when he got back, he'd get it wound up then, one way or another.

"Well, I'll be at home all Saturday and Sunday; but I'd certainly like to hear from you the minute you're back, so let me give you my home telephone number." He gave it to him, and Jeffries repeated it back slowly as he wrote it down. Then John Fowler's brain clicked up another notch, and he suggested quickly, "If you're back for the week-end, how about coming down to my house for lunch on Sunday? Get a bit of fresh air after all these cities and hotels—"

"Well—that's kind—it's most kind, but—"

"Trains go from Charing Cross to Tunbridge Wells. Only takes about three-quarters of an hour. You give me a ring, and I'll meet you at the station in Tunbridge Wells—we're a few miles out. Really, we'd be delighted to have you, we hardly see a moving figure down there in the—the outback."

Jeffries laughed. "I'd like to visit you, and if I can I will. I'll call you, eh?"

As he put the phone down in its cradle, John Fowler thought with faint disgust, hearing his own voice again in his ears, I was almost begging him. Pleading with him! As a matter of fact he'd liked Jeffries, what he'd seen of him, and the ogre image he had of him arose from nothing except the man's commercial power: still—

His internal phone buzzed, and he grabbed it. "Fowler."

It was the managing director. "What news of Jeffries, John?"

"Nothing firm yet, I'm afraid."

"You'd better get after him, hadn't you?"

Ah, thought John, the cracking of whips! He recoiled almost physically from the instrument in his hand.

"I've just been talking to him. He's flying to Glasgow, due back late on Saturday or early Sunday. He can't say anything till then."

"First thing Monday then, eh? We can't slip up on this, you know. Get on to him on Monday, nine o'clock, eh?"

"He's lunching with me on Sunday, at my home, if he's back in time. He's going to ring me at home as soon as he gets in, anyway. Short of flying up there with him, there's not much—"

"All right, John, all right!" The voice chuckled in his ear. "I expect you've got it all sewn up, eh?"

John Fowler set the phone down. He muttered, "I'd like to sew *you* up." He smiled to himself, thinking, In the old sailmaker fashion: a couple of fire-bars at the feet, good stout canvas, and the last stitch through the corpse's nose to make sure it's really dead . . .

*   *   *

The wind had dropped and for two mornings now there'd been no frost; today the sun was shining and there was a distinct feeling of spring in the air. The children were all outside, milling around on the lawn under the watchful eyes of Miss Wilmott and her colleagues. The teachers stood like sentinels around the perimeter, sniffing the fine, warm air with its scent of things growing, and they smiled when the children spoke to them.

"You mean the whole lot's coming?" Peter Wale was talking to Andrew about the birthday party he was giving on Saturday, the day after tomorrow. "Even Jeremy Clark?"

Andrew nodded gloomily. "He was the first to answer. He and Hilda Patterson. It's sickening."

"Well, you shouldn't have asked them."

Andrew shrugged. "My mother said I couldn't leave anyone out, except if they had measles or something, because I've been to all *their* parties."

"What's *that* got to do with it? They *asked* you, didn't they?" Peter sounded indignant.

"I know. But I'm not allowed to argue. Besides, they'll all bring presents, and I don't have to speak to the ones I don't like, so it doesn't really matter."

Peter Wale bent down to take hold of one end of a worm, which was poking out of a hole in the ground. He muttered fiercely, "Got you!" and pulled, to get it out of the ground, but the worm broke in two and he was left with only an inch of it in his fingers. He straightened up, and told Andrew, "I'll keep it in case I see a bird to give it to." They looked carefully all round, but there wasn't a bird in sight, not even a sparrow. Peter said to Andrew, "I bet your lion's hungry, shut up in that old stable all this time."

"It's not shut up," said Andrew irritably. "I told you, there's a big window thing it can jump out of when it wants to. My grandfather opened it, ages ago."

Peter Wale opened his hand and stared at the limp end of the worm. He said, "It'd be funny if it jumped out right in the middle of your birthday party, wouldn't it?"

"Nobody'd know. The window's right in the corner. It can come and go as it likes. Anyway, it's probably gone by now." In a way, he hoped it *had* gone; he knew it couldn't stay there for ever. But his relief would be tempered with sadness, he knew that too, if he found the stable empty.

Peter Wale suddenly grabbed Andrew's elbow with his free hand. He suggested excitedly, "Couldn't we have a look in there on Saturday?"

"How? My father won't let us play outside. He's said so. And if they saw us—"

"If they're all playing stupid games inside they won't know, if we're quick. We could just sneak out and look, couldn't we?"

They were all called in, then, because it was time for the afternoon class. Peter Wale had forgotten that he still had the worm in his hand; he put it down on his desk in the groove meant for pens and things, and poked it about with a pencil until Miss Wilmott noticed that he wasn't paying much attention. Suddenly she stopped talking, glared at him, and asked him what he was playing with. Peter pushed the bit of worm into his inkwell and held up the pencil for her to see.

"Do you mean this, Miss Wilmott?"

*   *   *

The next day, Friday, Andrew agreed to Peter Wale's suggestion that if they got a chance, during the party, they'd creep out and look inside the stable to see if the lion was still there. Andrew had lain awake for hours on Thursday night, thinking about it, and he'd decided that he'd quite like to have Peter Wale with him when he went down there and opened the stable door. He had to do it some time, and during the party might be as good a chance as he'd get.

It was really quite a relief to have come to this decision, and to know that he'd have someone with him.

He told Peter, "We'll come back by the garage, and if they've missed us we can say I've been showing you my new bicycle. I dare say you'd like to see it anyway, so we'll be telling the truth too. They can't kick up much fuss about a thing like that."

Peter Wale looked delighted. "When did you get a new bicycle?"

"I'm getting one for my birthday. I heard them talking about it."

IX

ANDREW STOOD at the window of his bedroom and watched the light grow across the hillside. With the daylight there was a mist that clung to the fields and thickened in the dip where the stream ran, so that the willows looked as if they were floating in soapy water. Andrew watched the hillside closely as the light increased, thinking that if the lion was still using the stable, going out at night to find its food and slinking back to hide up during the day, it would be at about this time that it would come back. But he saw nothing at all that moved, except for birds, pigeons and crows, starlings and magpies, and once a flight of wild duck which passed over on a dead-straight course like bombers on a dawn mission.

Well, he wouldn't be seeing the lion now that it was really daylight. It was cleverer than that, otherwise they'd have caught it long ago. If it was still using the stable, it would be in there by now, no doubt lying down and dropping off to sleep just as the rest of the countryside was waking up.

While he was dressing himself, Andrew suddenly began to wonder if his new bike might be downstairs in the house—the kitchen was the most likely place, if it was. They usually had any presents in the house, even outdoor things, for him to see when he first got up. Of course, since it was going to be a real bicycle, a boy's one and not the child's sort that he'd grown out of, they might have thought it was too big for that and left it in the garage. It was worth having a look, anyway.

He crept along the passage and into the bathroom, where he drew the curtains apart and pressed his face against the window to look down across that end of the garden into the paddock. It was all misty, damp-looking; he could see, over the top of the hedge, the roof of the stable and its corner and the door, which of course was still shut, as he'd left it in that breathless moment that seemed, now, like something that had happened six months ago. He'd made a habit, during the week, of coming to this window each morning and every afternoon as soon as he got back from school, to make sure that nobody had been down there and opened the door. He was sure nobody'd been there since the soldiers' first visit; they'd been here again, during the week and when he was at school, but his mother had told him all about it and they'd only searched the stream along its other bank, and the hedgerow of the lane; they'd looked into the garden from all round it, but they hadn't been inside.

While he was looking down into the paddock Andrew thought of another reason why the lion would certainly have to move away now, for its own safety: the frosts were over and the ground was getting soft. If the lion kept on using the stable, sooner or later they'd find its tracks and trail it back here after one of its nights out. Then they wouldn't even have to go into the stable: they could just wait outside with their guns and shoot it the next time it came out. Andrew stood at the window and shut his eyes and murmured, "God, please let us find the stable empty." He'd already decided that if it *was* empty, when he and Peter Wale looked inside, he was going to tell Peter that it had never been there, that he'd dreamt some of the story and made the rest up. It wouldn't be difficult to say, because it felt almost like that already: and Peter would believe it. They often made up stories to tell each other. He'd say to Peter, "I wanted to know if you'd be frightened to look inside."

His new bicycle was in the kitchen, propped against the table. It was marvellous. He hadn't really thought about it much, with so many other things in his mind, but when he saw it there, all new and shiny and strong-looking, a *real* bike that he'd be able to go for really long rides on, he felt quite stunned with excitement and he just stood in the doorway staring at it for quite a long time before he went right up to it and put his hands on it for the first time. The handlebars and wheel-rims were shiny steel and the rest of it was black with a red line along the bars of the frame and edging the mudguards. The saddle was smooth black leather; there was a bell, and a bracket for a lamp, and a special pump for the tyres, with the same red line along it, and behind the saddle there was a leather bag for tools. Andrew's fingers trembled as he undid the straps and took out the spanners and examined them; he put them back in the little tool-bag and fastened it up again.

He moved the bike away from the kitchen table, and mounted it, balancing by keeping his left hand on the edge of the table. The seat was at exactly the right height for him, so that his feet rested easily on the pedals. He turned them, backwards, listening to the dry singing noise the ball-race made as the pedals span. He was doing that when his father's voice came quietly from somewhere just behind him.

"Happy birthday, Andrew."

John Fowler was in pyjamas and dressing-gown. He must have crept down the stairs very quietly, on purpose, to surprise the boy when he heard him down there. He said now, "Many happy returns, old chap!" and he came into the kitchen soft-footed in his slippers and kissed Andrew on his head. "Like it?"

"Is it all right, Andrew?" Susan Fowler was down as well, also in her night clothes. She came in and kissed him too, and said "Happy birthday, darling." He hugged her, and saw his father smiling; he told them both, "It's super. Absolutely super!"

His father said, "We're going to get dressed now, but when I'm down, while your mother's making breakfast, I'll come out with you and you can ride it to the garage. H'm?"

Susan Fowler asked him, "What kind of eggs would you like for breakfast, Andrew?"

He said quickly, grinning, "Scrambled, please. With tomato sauce."

John Fowler shuddered. "I'll have scrambled too." They all said together, loudly, "And *no* tomato sauce!" It was an old joke and they'd laughed at it for years now; but there was more to it than that. It was Grandfather Kenney who had always had tomato sauce with his scrambled eggs, and Andrew had learnt that from him.

Susan said quickly, "Well, let's get on with it. There's masses to do."

While his parents were upstairs getting dressed, Andrew stood at the window in the study, watching two starlings fight over an old brown crust. It was a loaf, really, but hollow from the smaller birds who'd worked-out its insides. Eventually it broke in two, and the fight ended with each bird having a separate breakfast. Then his father came down and called Andrew; he opened the back door and let Andrew wheel the bike out on his own, not offering to help. Outside, John Fowler shut the door behind them and then looked round the garden and round the other side of the house: he came back and told Andrew, "All clear!" Andrew mounted his new bike and pedalled it to the garage; his father came more slowly, and then had to unlock the padlock on the door, and that gave Andrew time to ride around a bit on the concrete driveway. It was wonderful: when he could get out in the road it would be even better. He put the bike in carefully at the back of the garage—behind his father's car, which was safer than it would have been behind his mother's— and they left the door latched open and walked back to the house. John Fowler rested a hand on his son's shoulder, and Andrew felt mean to be keeping secrets from him. But he remembered how he'd blurted that out about the lion, to Peter Wale, when he hadn't meant to, and how afterwards he'd wished so strongly that he hadn't; so he kept his mouth shut and they walked along in silence.

After breakfast, as Susan had so much work ahead of her, Andrew and his father did the drying-up and made the beds. There was some shopping to be done, and John Fowler told the boy he could come along. Susan was going to be busy in the kitchen; she'd been making cakes and jellies and so on throughout the last two days, but apparently there was still a lot to do.

On the way to the garage they found Dingett, the gardener, digging over the vegetable beds again. With the ground so much softer he was finding it a lot easier than he had last week. When he saw them coming he straightened up, stuck his spade in the newly-dug earth and removed the splintery old pipe from his mouth.

"Mor'n, sir. They ain't found that ol' lion, then?"

"Morning. No, they haven't. It could be close by, you know; better keep your eyes open." He grinned at the old man.

Dingett tilted his head back and looked at John Fowler under half-lowered lids. He mumbled, "Reckon e's left the country, be now."

John Fowler laughed politely. But Dingett hadn't finished. "'Opped acrorss to Frarnce, oi reckon."

The shopping didn't take long. There was the bread to collect, and a large parcel of small rolls which Susan had ordered, and a few other things. John Fowler needed some tobacco, and he bought Andrew a bar of chocolate, which had disappeared before they got home.

The kitchen was so full of mixing-bowls and other equipment that there was nowhere to put their parcels down. Susan cleared a space; she told Andrew, "You've got chocolate all over your chin."

John Fowler asked her what they could do to help, and she said there were about thirty balloons to be blown up. They were in the cupboard in the study, and the string was in there too. Andrew and his father set about it systematically, first cutting off dozens of lengths of string and then sitting on the floor with all the stuff between them and blowing the balloons up as fast as they could; it was hard work and it took a lot of breath.

John Fowler was glad to have something to do; his mind wasn't on the party at all, it was on the phone call he hoped to get from that man Jeffries later in the day. One of the balloons burst, and he hardly noticed the bang; he just reached for another one and started blowing, wondering what Jeffries might have fixed up in Glasgow and whether he'd ring at all. It was just possible that if the deal went through, the full contract, they might offer him, John Fowler, a seat on the Board. It seemed too much to hope for and he was almost certain something would go wrong. Another balloon exploded in his face, and Andrew told him, "You're blowing them up too much. They don't have to be so big."

When it was all finished they went into the kitchen to ask Susan what they should do next; she said there wasn't anything, except to keep out out of her way. Later the dining-room would have to be cleared, but she wanted to be there to see to that and she wasn't ready yet.

"Can't we go out and have another look at my bike?"

"All right. Come on."

They went out. Dingett was still digging in the same bed. Andrew asked him, "Would you like to see my new bicycle?" The old man stopped work and stared at him with those piercingly blue eyes; then he grinned, showing the teeth that weren't his, and shuffled along behind them to the garage.

"Birthday, then?"

John Fowler nodded. "Eight." Andrew wheeled the bike out and displayed it proudly. He said, "It's a real boy's one." Dingett crouched down slowly, breathing hard and noisily; his eyes ran keenly over the shiny steel. He muttered, "Make 'em fancy, all right." He stood up, and told John Fowler, "'Ee want to ride around, oi'll watch 'un."

"*Can* I, Daddy?"

His father hesitated. "Well—I suppose you can. Not for long, though. When I call, you come straight in, eh?" He said to Dingett, "Mind you watch him, now." He stood beside the gardener and watched the boy mount his machine and start riding around on the concrete; then he walked off towards the back door of the house, looking all round the garden as he went. He felt he couldn't have refused Dingett's offer; but he was uneasy and wished the old man hadn't made it.

Andrew was thrilled to be on the bicycle. When he turned at the garage end and faced several yards of concrete driveway, he pushed down hard on the pedals and the machine leapt forward so powerfully that he had to brake hard in time to turn again. Out on the road it was going to be a dream to ride.

But after a few minutes he got tired of riding up and down in such a restricted space. He stopped, still on the bike but leaning with one hand on the corner of the garage, and he looked down towards the paddock gate. The cinders would be easy enough to ride on.

Dingett was back at his digging and he never looked up. It occurred to Andrew that he hadn't been told to stay on the concrete. He pushed off from the garage and started down the slope towards the gate; the tyres scrunched loudly on the cinders, and he hadn't counted on that. Dingett looked up at once.

"Don't ye go far, lad!"

Andrew didn't answer; it was hard going over the bumpy track, even though it was downhill, and he had to press hard on the pedals to stop the bike wobbling. At the gate he stopped, and got off. He could see the stable from here, and the door; he hadn't been so close to it for a week. Suddenly a dreadful thought came to numb him with disappointment: Dingett would be here all day! There were several vegetable beds that he hadn't dug yet, and he was double-digging, a slow process, trenching as he went. He'd be here this afternoon, still at it, and they wouldn't have a hope of getting past him . . .

Andrew walked back up the cinder track, pushing the bicycle. He didn't feel like going on riding, now. He pushed it into the garage and propped it against the back wall; when he came out, Dingett was leaning on his spade, watching him.

"You goin' in, then?"

Andrew nodded miserably. Dingett said, as he passed close to him, "Miss your grandad, I dare say?" The boy stopped, surprised at the question from that source. The gardener nodded slowly in a kind of sad approval. He muttered, "They don't make 'em like that no more."

Andrew knew that was true, in a way; but as Dingett had said it, the remark had seemed to be directed against his father. He turned his back on the old man and walked quickly into the house.

*　　*　　*

The children had been invited for half-past three, and at exactly that time the door-bell rang. Andrew was with his mother in the dining-room; the table had been pushed back against the end wall and the chairs set all round with their backs against the other walls so that the middle of the room was empty. A big cluster of balloons hung from the central light: reds, greens, blues and yellows: and the table was covered with plates of food and jellies which were the same colours as the balloons.

When the bell rang, Andrew said, "That'll be Jeremy Clark. I can't stand him." Susan Fowler glanced at him reprovingly, and beckoned him to come with her to the door.

A tall woman was waiting outside with a weedy boy holding one of her hands and a short, fat girl clasping the other. She smiled, and told Susan proudly, "I'm Mrs Clark and this is Jeremy. I've brought Hilda Patterson too, the sweet little thing. They live next door to us."

"How do you do?"

"They—I mean—you won't be letting them play in the garden, Mrs Fowler, will you? It is Mrs Fowler, isn't it?"

Susan shook her head. "No, I won't; and yes, it is."

Mrs Clark looked surprised, and giggled. She said, "You *are* rather—well, exposed, here, aren't you? I mean, there aren't any other houses — just fields — so I thought—"

"Of course." Susan reassured her, wishing she'd let the children come in and take herself off. "They'll be indoors all the time."

"Yes." The woman giggled again. "Well, I'll come back for them at—six, is it?"

Susan had arranged things so that the children would take their coats and outdoor shoes off in the study, and then go on into the sun-room, where she hoped they'd do most of their playing. Like the dining-room, it was decorated with balloons. Andrew soon gave up the chore of answering the door with his mother; he took up a position in the study, less to receive the guests than to receive the presents which each child brought and reluctantly handed over. Andrew just grabbed each little packet and took it into the sun-room to unwrap it; nearly every one contained a model car, match-box size; within ten minutes he had four tiny, identical Jaguars. The children arrived in a steady stream until the house seemed full of them and both the Fowlers were looking desperate: cars rolled up one after the other and fathers or mothers shoved their children in the door and tore away again with obvious relief. The children arrived in tense, nervous silence; shedding their coats, they burst into noisy abandon. Several of the mothers asked the same question that Mrs Clark had asked; Susan had the answer ready for them almost before they'd opened their mouths.

She said to John Fowler as she pushed past him, herding a new arrival to the study, "They must think we're nuts!"

Her husband glanced around him, and raised his eyebrows. "Are you sure we aren't?" The bell rang: Susan muttered something short under her breath, pushed the child she had with her into the sun-room, and hurried back to the front door. Outside it she found a tall, fair man with a small, pugnacious-looking boy.

The man said, "My name's Wale. This is Peter. You'll probably wish you hadn't asked him."

Susan laughed. She told him quietly, "When I told Andrew he could have a party, he said he only wanted Peter Wale. I had to make him ask all the others. You'll come back for him at six?"

"I'll bring a strait-jacket."

Later, in the kitchen, Susan Fowler told her husband, "There's a boy called Peter Wale—the one Andrew actually likes—"

"I know him. The only one who didn't bring one of those dreadful little cars."

"What did he bring? A cobra?"

"A water-pistol that holds a full half-pint. Andrew just used it on a child called Hilda."

"That's nice." Her mind wasn't on it. "I was going to say, his parents are nice. We should ask them down here for a drink or something."

"If they're so nice, why don't they ask us?"

She laughed. "You're just like Andrew!"

He didn't mind that kind of criticism. He didn't mind anything much, this afternoon, except whether Jeffries rang or didn't. He pulled Susan close to him, and kissed her; then he went back into the arena, and Andrew drew him aside.

"Is Dingett still here?"

"No. He pushed off after lunch. Why—did you want to ask him in for a jelly?"

Andrew had already plunged off towards Peter Wale; Susan came out of the kitchen to announce that they all had to go into the dining-room for tea. She didn't know that half of them were in there already, eating all the nuts and cherries off the cakes.

*   *   *

Andrew grabbed Peter Wale's elbow. There was a terrible volume of sound in the small room, and he had to yell in his friend's ear to make himself heard. "Ready, now? The stable?"

Peter Wale let go of a small boy's shirt-front, and nodded enthusiastically. Andrew bellowed, "We can use the side door: through the downstairs lavatory!" He led the way out, thrusting his guests aside with no hint of apology. But when they got to the lavatory, they found it was locked from the inside. Andrew whispered in Peter's ear, "We'll have to wait. Can't go through the kitchen, my mother's in there." But only a few seconds after he'd said that, he banged on the door and shouted, "Hurry up, whoever you are!"

The lock clicked almost at once, and his father towered over them in the doorway. Andrew apologised, blushing, while Peter Wale sniggered. John Fowler told them, "Go on in, for heaven's sake, before it's too late." He moved off towards the dining-room, and asked Peter as he passed him, "D'you shout at *your* father when he's in the lavatory?" Peter answered tersely, "Sometimes." John Fowler ambled away down the passage, shaking his head; but he was wondering whether he'd hear the telephone, if it rang, above this din.

The two boys went on into the cloakroom and shut the door, and Peter stood by it ready to stop anyone else who might try to get in, while Andrew unlocked the outer door and pulled it open. They went out quickly into the garden and shut the door behind them; they'd be able to get in again the same way, Andrew explained in a whisper, and if there happened to be someone sitting in there, well, they'd get a surprise, that was all. He added, "If it was Hilda Patterson, I'd push her right in."

"Couldn't," whispered Peter. "Her bottom's too fat."

Andrew led him right around the house, so that they wouldn't pass the kitchen window, where his mother might see them. They walked as quietly as they could, and bent down whenever they passed a window. At the dining-room window, though, Andrew stopped, and peered in before he crept by underneath it: his father was in there, finishing off the chocolate cake, all by himself. Andrew grinned as he stooped and led Peter, Red Indian fashion, to the corner of the house. They paused there, and Andrew pointed at the garage and at the paddock gate. He hissed, "Run, now. First to that corner, then down to the gate, and when we're over it we're safe 'cause we'll be behind the hedge. Ready?"

They ran as fast as they could; Peter cheated, and cut the corner, going slap over one of the beds that Dingett had been digging up. But they tumbled over the gate pretty well together, and a few seconds later they were crouching side by side on the other side of the hedge, in the paddock.

Andrew pointed at the stable. "There it is."

Peter stared at it. He muttered, "D'you think the lion's in there?"

Andrew frowned at him. He was the leader, and he felt it. He told Peter sternly, "That's what we've come to find out."

"What if it comes out at us?"

"You aren't *frightened*, are you?"

Peter's face went from white to red, and he pushed his jaw forward. "You saying I'm *frightened*?"

"You sound like it."

"Well, I'm not!"

Andrew was frightened, all right. He didn't admit it, even to himself; but he knew they had to get down to that stable and look into it right away. If they didn't do it at once, they'd soon think of some reason not to do it at all. He knew that without knowing why. It was the same feeling he'd had when the lion had stalked into the stable, a week ago; the door had had to be shut and he'd had to do it quickly, without waiting to think about it. That was the only way; he just knew it.

He whispered to Peter Wale, "Follow me, then. Keep on the grass, it's quieter. It might be asleep."

He could see the lion in his mind and memory. The size of it, the power. It would come up to his shoulder—its head would, that enormous head. The lion's eyes, now that he came to think about them and knew that in a few moments they might be staring straight into his, weren't in any way like Grandfather Kenney's eyes had been. They were slanted, slitted: evil. Grandfather Kenney's eyes had been the gentlest things he'd ever looked at. He hadn't considered this before, the raw savagery that was undoubtedly in the beast he'd been protecting. Things came clearly, suddenly, and when you least expected them: there were answers, and they came at moments such as this.

Not that there'd been moments like this before. Andrew felt his body shaking, a weakness in his legs. He didn't want to speak again because he knew his voice would be thin and trembling, not like his at all, and he didn't want Peter Wale to hear that and know that he was terrified. So he just jerked his head, and, bent double, began to creep down along the line of the hedge towards the stable.

X

JOHN FOWLER pressed the telephone receiver against his left ear and held his right hand across the other to shut out some of the noise from the next room. The telephone was in the study and he'd been standing right next to it when it had rung; he'd pushed all the children into the sun-room—Susan was in there with them—and shut the door. Even with the door shut, the noise they made was awful.

"Why, yes!" He shouted again, "I said *yes*: that's splendid! Look—my son's got a party going on—birthday—I can hardly hear myself, let alone you!"

At the other end, Jeffries laughed, and he began to shout too. He yelled, "Right then, Fowler: I'll call you from the station—Tunbridge Wells—when I get there. That right?"

"Fine!" In that next room, balloons were going off like machine-guns. "I'll get there within ten minutes of your call."

He felt as if he'd been struck deaf. Jeffries' voice came faintly in his ear, "Okay then. Look forward to seeing you."

"Tell me one thing—did you tie anything up in Glasgow?"

"Did the *what?*"

"I mean, will we get—"

Apart from the noise, something had got hold of the arm that held the telephone; something that gripped it, swung on it, tugged it away from his face. Bewildered and furious, shouting his last question into empty air, John Fowler twisted round and looked down in absolute amazement at Peter Wale.

Peter Wale seemed to have gone mad. He was hanging on to that arm with one hand and actually hitting out at Andrew's father with the other: he was scarlet in the face and screaming, and tears were showering down his face. John Fowler, now as alarmed as he was surprised, dragged the instrument back close to his mouth and yelled into it, "Good-bye! See you tomorrow!"

Peter Wale, who'd thought he was losing the fight, had shifted his other hand now and flung all his small weight on to that one arm of John Fowler's: the telephone receiver fell, clattered against the wall on the end of its cord: he shouted down at the demented child, "What on earth—"

"The lion! I told you, *the lion!* In the stable! *Andrew's in the stable with the lion!*"

*　　*　　*

John Fowler never remembered feeling any surprise that the outside door of the cloakroom was standing wide open. He never remembered any lucid thought at all: only blind, wild panic. He crashed out through that door and ran harder and faster than he'd done in at least a dozen years. From the door he ran in a straight line across a rockery and a short flight of steps and over the vegetable beds and then over the paddock gate in a flying leap which at any other time he couldn't possibly have managed: Peter Wale's shouts rang in his ears and in front of him down the slope the stable door stood ajar. He crashed into it full tilt, flinging it back with his weight and the momentum of his headlong rush: in the stable's gloom he cannoned into his son and the two of them went down sprawling across the lion.

The boy, and the lion, were under him, and he felt as if he'd been hit by a heavy truck. The boy fought, struggling out from under him, silent except for his choking, panting breath.

The lion was dead. It was dead, and it stank. Rising slowly to his feet, his eyes on the huge, outspread animal, his right arm reaching out blindly for Andrew, who'd squirmed aside and got clear of both his father and the lion, John Fowler realised that the animal must have been in here, dead, for at least a week. You didn't have to be a zoologist to know that: all you needed was a nose.

Andrew had taken hold of the hand that was reaching out for him: he still hadn't said a word. John Fowler told him, panting, "Let's get out in the air."

Outside, he crouched down in front of his son, holding him by the shoulders and looking him over carefully for any signs of damage. The boy's face was deathly white, but otherwise he seemed to be unhurt. John Fowler pulled him close, and hugged him; he thought, *Thank God. Oh, I mean it, God: thank you!* Moving back, still holding the boy in front of him, he mustered enough breath to speak.

"Did you know it was in there?"

Andrew shook his head. "No, but—I let it in. I opened the door because someone had shut it, and when I was up there"— he pointed at the gate—"I saw it come out of the stream and walk in."

"You shut the door again?"

The boy nodded. His father asked, "Why?"

"I don't know. . . . I didn't want them to shoot it."

"You didn't—yes, I remember that. I suppose you can't tell me *why* you felt like that about it?"

"I thought—you see, I saw it on the hill, before, at night from my window." Andrew's eyes searched his father's face, looking for signs of anger or understanding. He said, "It was at night, a week ago. It stopped and looked straight at me. I thought—"

His voice faltered and his lips trembled. John Fowler said quickly, seriously, "You thought it was your friend. That's why you didn't want it shot?"

Andrew nodded. John Fowler didn't ask any more questions; he could sense the rest, an emotion and a kind of blind sincerity which wouldn't stand up to questions because it couldn't be matched in words or touched by logic. He only knew that his son was alive in the plain, ordinary, glorious sense and in several other ways as well, and beyond all that—although also it was because of it—that he was strangely, fiercely proud of him.

He stood up, and told Andrew, "There's a big open window in there. The lion could have got in that way, after the door was shut. We'll let them think that's how it got in, shall we?"

Andrew just stood there, looking up at him. "We'll tell your mother the truth, because we don't have secrets from her. But everyone else: it won't be telling a lie, old chap, we'll just let them work it out for themselves."

Andrew nodded, and began to smile. Then they heard a sound up by the gate, and they both looked round and saw Peter Wale clambering over it. John Fowler called, "It's all right—it's been dead for ages!" He went back to the doorway, and peered into the stable. He said, as Peter joined them, wiping his eyes and sniffing, "Phew, what a smell! You all right now, Peter?"

"Yes, thank you. I'm sorry, I meant to tell you it seemed dead, but I wasn't sure."

"It's dead, all right. . . . But you were right to come for me." The smell of the dead lion drifted out to them, and he told his son, "We'll have to get this place properly cleaned out, now. Fumigated. I'll get someone to come and do it, next week. Then we'll find you a pony. It's time you had one."

Peter stared at Andrew with his mouth open, and Andrew stared wildly at his father. It was a bit much, all at once. John Fowler said, "Well, we'd better go on up now, and tell your mother. No, let the other children go home first. Then I'll ring Constable Williams for someone to come and take it away. And the army . . . Andrew: tell Peter how the lion must have got in there, will you? Be sure he understands."

John Fowler turned, and started up towards the house, walking not hurriedly but in long, easy strides that took him rapidly up the cinder track to the gate into the garden.

So the lion had been lying there, putrefying, for at least several days. Well, it was old: the major had mentioned that. Old, and probably sick. It had crept into the stable when Andrew had let it in; the boy could hardly have known it was only looking for a place to lie down and die, somewhere out of the frosts and the bite of the north wind and away from yapping dogs.

John Fowler frowned to himself, thinking that the few people who'd said they'd seen it—except for Mrs Hailey, who undoubtedly had—were going to look pretty silly now. They'd have a hard time of it in their villages: particularly the woman canvasser. And several farmers, who'd perhaps liked the idea of seeing their names in print and their faces on the Telly, would have to revise their ideas of what was dogs' work and what wasn't: or even of how many lambs had been born in the first place. And incidentally, they'd have to do something, now, about those dogs. They'd have to do it themselves, without the East Loamshires' help. The East Loamshires would be taking off for Cyprus.

John Fowler smiled to himself, imagining what Major Willesley would have to say if he ever knew that his Company had been held back for a week because an eight-year-old boy thought a lion was his friend. Well, he wouldn't know. Nobody would . . .

* * *

Andrew watched him go. He was thinking less about the promise of a pony than about the way his father had come hurtling down in a blind, pounding charge when he'd thought the lion was alive and dangerous. Thinking about that, the boy saw his father reach the gate and climb swiftly over it and stride on towards the house; he watched him go, and as he pulled himself out of his thoughts and memories and set off up that way himself, it began to dawn upon him—in a surge of happiness so sheer that it was stunning, overwhelming—it burst upon him suddenly that, after all, not all the lions were dead.